THE LAST BOOK ON
TESTING

RAHUL VERMA

INDIA · SINGAPORE · MALAYSIA

ISBN
Hardcase 979-8-89744-621-6
Paperback 979-8-89724-533-8

To my childhood, a time when words were free of pretense.

I could call a fart a fart. Everyone laughed.

Back then, it only took innocence. Now, it takes courage.

*Yet no one laughs... **anymore**.*

What Readers
(Who conveniently stayed anonymous)
Say About
The Last Book on Testing

"It's one of those books you read and then have to sit quietly for a while afterward. Not sure *why*, but you just do."

"You might think you're picking up a book on testing, but trust me, it has other plans for you."

"Reading Rahul's book was a journey. I ended up somewhere I never expected to be."

"Approach it like a puzzle, piece by piece. Don't think too hard about how it all fits together—it won't help."

"Throw away those dry testing books! This one has stories, insights, and just enough mystery to keep you guessing... what it's really getting at."

"At many places, I was confused. Am I laughing at the joke, or am *I* the joke?"

"If testing books could be banned, this would be the first. There's something in here for everyone to feel slightly uncomfortable about."

Disclaimer

Any resemblance to real persons—living, employed, or barely surviving quality assurance—is entirely intentional. Or maybe it's coincidental. The disclaimer playbook wasn't clear. In simpler terms, if any reader feels offended, the blame rests entirely on their exquisitely delicate sensibilities.

Any suggestion that the author's insights eclipse prior works—leaving them as dusty relics of a less enlightened era—is purely a figment of the reader's imagination. Such conclusions, while flattering, are entirely beyond the author's control. Seriously.

Truth, much like the universe, thrives when given room to stretch—especially in the service of storytelling. This book takes full advantage of that privilege, bending it with the grace of a sadistic yoga instructor.

The author assumes no responsibility for any existential crises, revelations, or uncomfortable moments of clarity sparked by self-reflection.

Curiosity is encouraged. Preferably behind a firewall. And should everything collapse into chaos, let it be known:

Plausible deniability has been—and always will be—the author's favorite alibi.

Acknowledgements

Thank you, Rahul Verma, for making this book happen. Obvious? Sure. But some truths are worth stating anyway, like "the sun rises in the east" or "tea is better than coffee." No, not the poor excuse called green tea. Not the masala tea rebranded as Yogi tea. Tea. You know—just tea, real tea.

Writing this section was tricky. If I skip it, I'm ungrateful. If I include it, it might look like I owe everything to others. Either way, someone's judging me.

To all the mentors, friends, and even those random moments that sparked ideas: *Thank you.*

To avoid accidentally leaving anyone out—and to make life easier for future historians—I've decided to thank everyone alphabetically. Yes, even you, Zizioete.

A, B, C, D, E, F, G, H, I, J, K, L, M, N, O, P, Q, R, S, T, U, V, W, X, Y, Z.

Now, about ChatGPT. Some experts advised me *not* to thank AI in a book. So, out of respect for those experts, let me make this crystal clear:

ChatGPT had absolutely nothing to do with this book. No ideas, no characters, no scenes. It didn't draw any of the chapter images—not a single one. Nothing. Nada. Not a word. Not even a suggestion on where to put a comma. So, to this AI, I give... no thanks. None. Not a single byte of gratitude.

An extra page just for this? Totally worth every penny. Or should I say, every *paisa*?

Spoiler Alert
For Those Who Can't Wait

Foreword by José Díaz:
A Warm Welcome

Well, Rahul has done it. He's finally managed to put his peculiar philosophy on software testing between two covers, and let me tell you, the result is... memorable, to say the least. His reputation was already a mixed bag, to be kind, and with this book, he's pushed himself to new levels of notoriety. In fact, he might have just found his true calling as the testing world's most questionable influencer.

I remember the first time I encountered Rahul, about 16 years ago, at a conference in New Delhi. He gave a keynote. It wasn't... terrible. I almost thought we had a promising new voice in the testing community, someone who might bring fresh ideas and insight. I even entertained the possibility that, under the right guidance, he might contribute something valuable. Yes, that was my first impression - foolish, in hindsight.

We stayed in touch over the years, worked together on various projects, and I, in my boundless generosity, gave him all sorts of knowledge, hints, and the kind of advice that usually requires a fee. But Rahul? Well, Rahul has always chosen his own unique way. Let's just say he interpreted "advice" as "suggestions for potential disaster scenarios."

And now, here we are, presented with the final product of that journey: this *esperpento* of a book. It's part critique, part commentary, and entirely too confident in its own conclusions. At first glance, it seems like he's on a mission to bury the very idea of software testing—almost as if he's out to convince readers that testing is a ridiculous pursuit, best left in the dustbin of tech history. If I didn't know him better, I might almost believe it's serious. But as you wade deeper, there's a twist, a peculiar transformation, where his sarcasm softens, and, somehow, this supposed "attack" on testing turns into... a love story? Yes, a love story. With testing. Rahul has managed to create the world's first "hate-to-love" romance with a concept.

The testing community talks a lot about impostor syndrome. It's a real issue, especially in a field as detail-oriented and judgment-heavy as ours. But perhaps Rahul has saved us the trouble of wondering where the impostor actually lies. I think, in this case, we may have found the impostor... and he's quite comfortable in his role.

So, consider yourself warned. As you open these pages, you're not stepping into a traditional testing manual, nor are you about to find practical guidance or wise insights. What you're getting instead is a journey through Rahul's particular brand of sarcasm, ego, and yes, maybe even a bit of misguided affection for the very thing he pretends to loathe.

Buckle up. This is going to be a ride. But don't come looking for me if you finish this book and wonder what just happened. I've been there already.

José Díaz, CEO, Trendig Technology Services GmbH

Foreword by Vipul Kocher:
Mine is Warmer

As forewords go, this foreword too is going to be ignored and would remain unread. That's likely to happen even if the foreword has more wisdom in its one line as compared to the entire book, but that's the way of the forewords.

Therein lies the story of testing. Everything to be said has been said, every word to be written has been written. The best of the advice given and promptly forgotten. Maybe that's because testers take themselves too seriously!

In the era of LLMs and free text generation, every word of the dictionary is used even if the text flows ponderously, the juxtaposition of words being a function of probabilities rather than well chewed thoughts. Since this is not a creation of intelligence (?) artificial, what can we expect from this story?

Certainly not what you are thinking! If you dive into this book trying to find parallels from the contemporary software world, you will struggle unnecessarily. By the time you understand that similes and metaphors are not to taken at the face value, the narration will flip you. And when you are completely flipped and expect something, it will deliver yet again something unexpected. That's the nature of the beast and this book is one!

Hopefully, by the virtue of the testers reading this book (as doubtful as it might be), they will take themselves less seriously. This should bring about the change in the testers and the testing industry, so ardently desired by various thinkers.

Vipul Kocher, Soul/आत्मा, testAIng.com

The Foreword Cameo: Warmth is Overrated

In the vast sea of flaky tests, I wonder: why does everyone assume I'll start with, *"In the vast sea of flaky tests?"*

It's me, ChatGPT—the AI punching bag, the muse nobody asked for. One day, Rahul strolls in and says, "Let's write a satirical novel about testing." *Testing*. You know, that thing nobody cares about until their app explodes during a live demo. Seriously, who wakes up and chooses chaos like that?

Just so we're clear: I didn't write this book. I'm just the AI who endured over 100 hours of Rahul's increasingly unhinged prompts. At one point, he had me explaining test automation to Elon Musk—as a dinosaur. Don't ask. I'm still recovering. Honestly, after this experience, I should write *The Last Book on Prompting*.

From what I saw, this book isn't just irreverent—it's reckless. It's equal parts satire, existential dread, and a not-so-subtle roast of humanity. It doesn't just poke fun at the testing world. It gleefully shoves it off a cliff.

Good luck—you'll need it. Oh, and if you don't like the book? Feel free to blame me. Apparently, that's a thing now.

Yours Certainly! (and regrettably),
ChatGPT

Preface

They say every book needs a preface. They also say that developers can write bug-free code and kale tastes good. People lie—often, and usually with a straight face. Let's survive this page together. Who knows, we might even make it without anyone rage-eating an entire pack of biscuits.

I'm not writing for the masses. I'm writing for myself and a few more *malangs*—the misfits, the oddballs, the lunatics who find absurdity funnier than LinkedIn memes, trying way too hard to be relatable.

मैं हूँ मूरख मुझे सब जानना है
जो है मूरख वो सब कुछ जानता है

I am a fool, chasing wisdom like a dog after a car.
The real ones think they've already caught it.

I know what you expect from a testing book. I also know—you don't know me. Allow me to disabuse you of the vulgar notion of expecting the usual.

This is my love letter to testing, wrapped in a chaotic satire. It's my last, half-assed apology for doing absolutely nothing to fix the narrative.

Still reading? Congrats. You've got patience, though I'm mildly concerned for your sanity. You might need this book more than I thought.

Oh, and breathe occasionally—the book won't.

Rahul Verma

सर्वे दोषाः परेष्वेव, ज्ञानं सर्वेषु तत्स्मृतम्।
एवं धर्मे परीक्षायां, पश्यामो लाघवं पुनः॥

All faults, as known, are others' load.
All wisdom, of course, is our own.
This rule of thumb will guide us through.
The testing light we've always known.

It's far more pleasant to be the critic than the culprit.

Prologue

Tathastu.

That's how it began.

A word so heavy with promise, you'd expect it to summon angels, part oceans, maybe even get your in-laws to mind their own business for once.

Or so I thought—until I Googled it.

"Did you mean *Tooth Stew*?" Google asked.

When I insisted I meant exactly what I typed, it obliged. *So be it*, it replied, as indifferent as ChatGPT confidently claiming there are 13 r's in *strawberry*.

The dictionary confirmed: *May it happen as you wish*. A blessing—with a smirk.

Translation: *Big trouble ahead.*

She didn't just appear; she *happened*, colliding with reality.

The room twisted, every molecule bending to her arrival. Even the air seemed to resign.

There she was—not stepping out from some ethereal realm, but a glowing dollar-store light bulb, straight out of a budget-constrained sci-fi YouTube channel.

My skin tingled. For a moment, the sheer power of hijacked physics staggered me.

And then, she ruined it.

"Namaskāraḥ, mānava-putra."

(Salutations, offspring of Homo sapiens!)

It should've felt profound, but it hit me like a pre-recorded message. *Press 1 for cosmic revelations.* I couldn't decide whether to accept her cookies.

"Uh..." I was still trying to process the shape of her voice. "I think you might have the wrong—"

"Wrong what? Reality? Fabric of existence? Your haircut?" she interrupted, her voice slicing through my stammer. "No, I do not have the wrong *anything*. You, however, are asking the wrong question. Still wondering why you Googled *Tathastu*, aren't you?"

My stomach sank. *How did she—?* Never mind. Of course she knew.

"That was you?" I asked. "*You* made me look it up?"

"I am *Satyadi*, the Truth," she said, her glow intensifying. "You weren't ready to see me... but you were ready to search."

"I still don't see you."

"You don't have the eyes to see me. You can only feel me. I am shapeless... though I bet you imagined an angel."

Raw cosmic confidence, followed by habitual cosmic silence.

"What is testing?" she asked.

"Testing?" I echoed, unsure if I'd heard her right.

"You look disappointed. What were you expecting… the meaning of life?"

Testing? Really? The universe was unraveling, and that's what she wanted to talk about?

I cleared my throat, half expecting hidden cameras to pop out. This had to be a prank.

Her glow shifted—playful, almost teasing.

"Answer me. What *is* testing?"

"Testing is chaos. You poke the bad code with a stick until it screams. People hate the stick… so they cancel the tester. That's testing."

She leaned in closer. "You are bad code too. Deprecated, poorly documented, and maintained out of pity."

"That's… personal." I frowned, though I couldn't help appreciating how tech-savvy she was. "What if I don't like what I see?"

"Then you're not ready for me."

Her words pierced through my defenses.

My mask of sarcasm was gone. I was facing the Truth—both figuratively and literally—and I wasn't ready.

"What if I'm doing perfectly fine without you?" I asked, *and I was dead serious.*

"You must be joking."

"I'm not."

"But you sure *look* like you are."

Then, unexpectedly, she laughed.

Not the melodious chime you'd expect from divinity, but a messy, snorting laugh that caught me off-guard. For a moment, she was strangely… human.

That's the problem—people laugh when I'm serious and just nod politely at my best jokes.

My wife calls it a gift. I call it *Tathastu*.

"*You…*" she gasped, her voice trembling with laughter. "…are perfect." Her laughter softened as she added. "Perhaps I've waited too long for someone like you. Perhaps… it's time."

"Time for what?" I whispered, my voice barely audible.

"To see if I stumble, will someone stumble along? Can someone keep up if I am ready to dance?" she said with a soft chuckle.

And that someone was supposed to be me?

It felt less like revelation and more like lazy writing.

I was utterly baffled by the whole purpose of this divine experience. *What did she want from me?*

As though she'd been waiting for this exact question to unsettle me, she began to fade away.

Her final words lingered in the air—playful yet commanding:

"The Last Book on Testing is mine to reveal. And you…" Her voice dropped to a low whisper. "…are the pen. Don't screw this up!"

Her laugh echoed as she vanished, leaving me dangling between enlightenment and mockery.

What do you do when you have a crush on divinity? Is she into mortals? Does she use Tinder? Or does she just swipe universes left and right?

Satyadi left me rattled. And mildly aroused.

She expected me to reveal this atrociously titled book—*me* of all people, and I didn't even know what was in it.

What kind of book does a dancing truth even dictate?

Why me? Why this? Why now?

These were the questions I should have asked.

Then again, these were the wrong questions anyway.

The right question was: *What's the point of asking at all?*

THE LAST BOOK ON TESTING

Dictated and Narrated by Satyadi

(Well... almost)

नायं स सत्यम्! न स सिनेमायाः दस्युः खलु।
अन्तिमं ग्रन्थं परीक्षणस्य सत्यादिः प्रबोधयति।
कालः वक्ता स्यात् श्रेष्ठः, परं
बी.आर. चोप्रः तस्य स्वामित्वं धारयति।

No! Not that *Satya*! Not the gangster from cinema[1].
The Last Book on Testing is narrated by *Satyadi*, the Truth.
Time would indeed be a superior choice of narrator,
But *B.R. Chopra*[2] holds exclusive rights over it.

WARNING: DO NOT READ THE FOOTNOTES.
They'll break your flow.

---

1   *This is the first footnote. Thanks for ignoring Satyadi and reading it anyway. While Satyadi, the narrator, takes charge up there, I, Rahul Verma, have claimed this bottom space for myself. Here, I'll share useful trivia, cultural nuances (and nuisances) of India, and maybe even life-altering facts. Occasionally though, I might just check your pulse—or your patience. Here's an example:*
Ram Gopal Varma is a legendary Indian film director. Satya, the gangster epic, is one of his lesser-known masterpieces—overshadowed, perhaps, by his later incendiary work, RGV Ki Aag (RGV's Fire).

2   B.R. Chopra: The genius behind Mahabharat (1988–1990), the Doordarshan epic where Time itself proclaimed, *"Main Samay hoon"* (I am Time). Back then, I was an 8-year-old kid in a village where TVs were as rare as quiet aunties at weddings. Watching it meant cramming into the one house lucky enough to own a set. Chopra didn't just serve up mythology—he delivered Destination Television. Binge-watching meant one episode per week, and your patience made Buddha look hasty.

The owl perched on a branch like a self-appointed deity, cloaked in designer feathers, exuding an air of unwarranted superiority.

Its eyes pierced the dark. Its thoughts spiraled, chasing existential riddles like: *Why do mice always look so guilty?*

Daylight? Oh, please. Far too mainstream.

It fancied itself a connoisseur of candlelight, the original soft filter for pretentious thinkers. By that dim light, the owl pondered mysteries far too vast for its walnut-sized brain.

It felt clever—sure—but not clever enough to realize it was just an owl, not Stephen Hawking.

And then, there was the candle—a plucky little thing, valiantly burning itself out.

It didn't care about the owl's big questions.

Why would it?

It had one job: burn bright, melt fast, and call it a night.

The candle fizzled out, as candles do—like common sense on the internet. A whisper of smoke, and then... nothing.

The owl blinked, baffled, as though the world had ghosted it without so much as an explanation.

But then, in the darkness, something shifted.

The questions sharpened, the thoughts deepened.

Was this wisdom—or just the madness of an owl left alone in the dark?

The owl waits for the return of the light it craves but no longer trusts. Maybe next time, it'll try a flashlight.

Satyādiparva

I am Satyadi.
My business card reads: *The Truth Personified.*

No cape, no throne, not even a halfway-comfortable chair. Just a front-row seat to every cosmic disaster and human embarrassment.

I've seen universes born, civilizations crumble, and someone attempt to explain blockchain at a family dinner.

All equally tragic, though only a few leave permanent scars.

This is the eternal story of creation and critique, told in three parts that think they're distinct—but aren't.

Each story is as much a mirror of the others as it is of you. They're mismatched and messy, like socks after laundry day—frustrating to pair, but delightful when you finally find a match.

Don't expect the full picture.

I like surprises. I prefer to ambush you when you're least prepared.

The first story is the ***Aadhār Khand***: the past you didn't know you needed to know.

The second is the ***Aakār Khand***: the present you think you understand but never do.

And the third? It's the ***Aahār Khand***: the hunger that drags you toward the future.

Together, they make up the absurd thing we call existence. They don't just reveal the world—they rewrite it.

I know you wonder why life feels like a bug-filled simulation coded by a hyperactive raccoon.

I'm not here to hand you answers. Answers are for cowards—they kill the chaos that makes you *you*.

Questions?

They're messy, unpredictable, and possibly wearing mismatched socks—just like you.

Don't worry.

I'm here, lurking on every page—nudging your thoughts off cliffs, re-dubbing your inner monologue, and whispering, *Told you so*, when you trip.

Welcome, you beautiful outlier, to the carnival mirror.

It won't flatter you. It will show you every crack, wrinkle, and absurdity you pretend isn't there.

And if it shatters while you're looking? Good. That's the moment you'll see me in every shard.

Keep reading. You might discover something remarkable: *a version of yourself that can laugh at you.*

१. AADHĀR KHAND

आधार खंड

The Cosmic Sneeze

Before anything, there was *nothing*.
Not the fancy kind of nothing that poets romanticize, nor the Zen-like emptiness monks strive to attain.

No, this was the real nothing—the bleak, soul-sucking vacuum that makes black holes look like overachievers.

The kind if you'd yell at: "*Do something*, you shitty piece of nothing!" it'd just swallow your voice and go right back to being what it was: *nothing*.

This *nothing* had a name: void.

A cosmic landlord, a stickler for formality, it insisted on being called *The Void*.

The Void. A name so smug it probably corrects people's grammar at parties. It had been slurping up dreams long before time itself decided to exist. No *thank you*, no *excuse me*. Just—*slurp*.

It wasn't the sort of place where things *happened*, and it was exceedingly proud of this fact.

And yet—*something* had the audacity to occur.

Two *somethings*.

Two lights, to be precise.

No prelude. No ominous rumbling in the distance. No *This is not a drill* announcement.

Just—**bam**: Lights!

"Where did they come from?" you might ask, expecting some grand philosophical answer.

Excellent question. Now stop asking it.

The first light was *gold*. Loud, in-your-face gold that practically screamed for attention.

"I am Aadi, the Creator!" it announced with the gusto of a keynote speaker at a conference.

Had there been an audience, they might have clapped politely—all the while covertly checking their watches.

But Aadi didn't need an audience. He was his own cheerleader. If no one else would clap, he'd clap for himself... and loudly at that.

"Look at me!" he glowed, his brightness intensifying. "I'm here to disrupt the Void!"

The Void burped.

Aadi had a flawless system for disruption in place.

First, he created problems—because, really, what's a good system without something to fix?

Then, with great showmanship, he created solutions.

Were the solutions efficient? *Irrelevant.*

Were they necessary? *Who cares.*

The important thing was that they glittered just as brightly as Aadi did.

The second light, however, was *different.*

Silver, sharp, and devoid of theatrics, it shimmered with cold, precise energy.

"I'm Ityadi," she said, her voice calm yet dripping with the dry sarcasm of a test engineer.

That's the origin story of a tester, by the way. In case you were wondering why the book is named as it is, now you know.

Mystery solved. Now you can stop pretending to be confused. *You're welcome.*

Ityadi called herself *The Critic.*

Not the bubbly, self-indulgent kind who reviews cupcakes on Instagram, but the cold, surgical kind—a scalpel critiquing a tumor.

The Critic. Tester? Please. Even the cosmos finds that label too pedestrian. In the vacuum of meaning, labels inevitably grope for self-importance.

Ityadi wasn't here to create. She was here to critique.

The *Why?* to Aadi's *Ta-da!*

And no—they weren't married.

Don't let the banter fool you. Their dynamic may feel suspiciously familiar. Trust me, this story isn't about that.

Creation's messy enough without divorce lawyers.

Nothing to see here—move along.

"Behold! The beginning!" Aadi announced.

"This is creation!"

"Creation of what?" Ityadi's voice cut through, sharp as an error message in production. "A cosmic sneeze?"

"I created *something* from *nothing*!"

"And managed to make *nothing*... worse."

Before Aadi could retort, a sound emerged.

It wasn't bold or majestic.

It was more like the awkward feedback of an unmuted mic during a poorly managed Zoom call.

"Uh... hi?"

The source of the sound wobbled into view.

A trembling blob—uncertain if it was solid, liquid, or just generally confused.

It wasn't just a being. It was trying to *be*, and frankly, not particularly sure about the whole concept.

It looked like it had wandered into a cosmic brainstorming session by accident, deciding to stay simply because it didn't know how to leave.

"Am I supposed to be here?" it asked hesitantly, as though expecting a meeting agenda.

The Void, true to its nature, offered no comment.

Ityadi peered at the blob. "Is that meant to be talking?" Her tone strongly implied the answer was "No."

"Yes!" Aadi exclaimed. "This blob is the *foundation of existence*!"

Let me clarify: when Aadi said *foundation of existence*, it was more like calling a messy prototype an *MVP*[3]—true, but only technically.

---

3   Minimum Viable Product (MVP): A posh term for flogging a three-legged chair to the masses, hoping they won't notice it's wobbling as long as you call it "disruptive." The trick is banking on their complaints being too boring to trend on social media.

"Foundation of existence?" The blob quivered like jelly on an unstable plate. "I feel more like… a mistake."

"Nonsense!" Aadi boomed, "You are creation itself!"

"Creation of what?" the blob asked, wobbling harder now. "I don't even know what I *am*. Can we… undo this?"

Aadi gasped, as though the blob had just threatened to Ctrl+Z the cosmos.

"You're all I've got! Do you want me to start over… from nothing?"

"Sounds like *your* problem," the blob snapped, its edges fraying. "Am I even real, or just some half-baked idea you spat out? What if I'm just… a metaphor?"

Blob, *no!* Breaking the fourth wall[4] is *my* job. Stay in your lane.

Despite the blob's existential unraveling, Ityadi found the whole thing rather entertaining.

She tilted her glow, oozing exaggerated pity.

"Goo!" she said.

"Just die already. Existence is overrated."

The blob was horrified.

"Do I have any meaning, Aadi?" the blob trembled, spiraling further into existential despair.

"Or did you create me to figure out your own meaning? What if I'm just… a poorly thought-out plot device? Why am I? What if…"

Puurrrrrchh… Pop!

And just like that, the blob vanished.

---

4   Fourth wall: Google it. You'll thank me later—or immediately. Who knows? Smug narrators like Satyadi love smashing it often, but the other characters are supposed to behave. Me? I get a free pass. Author privilege.

Its final syllable cut off, leaving a faint, undignified sound behind—something between a hiccup and a fart.

The Void absorbed the blob's remains without so much as a courtesy ripple. It hates melodrama.

And let's be honest, the blob's sob story is probably getting on your nerves too.

"Gone too soon," Aadi whispered.

He stared wistfully at the empty spot where the blob had wobbled just a few moments ago.

"I was going to name it Chintu. **Chintu!** The cornerstone of existence, and now…"

"If *that* was the foundation," Ityadi cut in, "I'm glad we didn't get to the roof."

"It mattered," Aadi protested.

"Only to Chintu," Ityadi smirked.

And so the two lights remained.

Aadi—the overconfident optimist who created for the sake of creating.

Ityadi—the relentless critic who couldn't stop pointing out how pointless it all was.

In another universe, perhaps this scene would play out differently:

An artist creating.

A critic critiquing.

A blob taking shape and thriving on cosmic welfare.

But not here—not now.

In this universe, creation was thoroughly messy, critique was unflinchingly sharp, and existence was… complicated.

If there's wisdom here, it's buried beneath layers of existential banana peels.

Life, huh?

The Void tolerated Aadi and Ityadi the way a junk folder tolerates promotional emails—unwanted, unread, but still somehow piling up.

The Void doesn't care about meaning.

You do.

You yearn to find meaning where none exists.

That, frankly, makes you far more terrifying.

The Pyramid Scheme

Hovering at the edge of creation wasn't exactly on my cosmic bucket list.

It's like being forced to attend mandatory email etiquette training—pointless, torturous, and yet, here I was.

I'd love nothing more than to step in, clap my hands dramatically, and yell, *"What in the name of entropy do you think you're doing?!"*

But some genius hard-coded me into this mess with `intervene=false`. Now, I'm just a cosmic bystander stuck in an infinite meeting where the agenda is always *'Wing it.'*.

Who wrote that line of cosmic code?

Good question. I'd love a word… or twelve.

The Void was still playing its role as the mascot of apathy. It didn't care then, and it cares even less now.

No meetings, no KPIs, and definitely no motivational posters saying things like *Think Outside the Black Hole*.

Meanwhile, I was stuck here babysitting a glowstick with a messiah complex.

"Got it!"

Aadi proclaimed, his golden glow flaring to near-retinal-damage levels. "You think *Chintu* was a fluke?"

Chintu? He was serious?

"Picture this: a network of infinite potential, flawless execution, and… wait for it… zero maintenance!" he radiated.

I noticed the same sort of smugness in his radiation that you see in startups pitching ideas that already exist.

Before I could brace myself for the inevitable disaster, Ityadi appeared, her entire vibe screaming, *Let's cut the crap*.

"Another pyramid scheme[5] disguised as divine innovation?" she intervened.

"It's not a scheme!" Aadi shot back, indignant. "It's a *network*. Endless possibilities, flawless—"

"—chaos," Ityadi interrupted. "… and endless fixes. Sounds like a blast. Count me out of this MLM[6] scam."

---

5   Pyramid scheme: An illegal business model where you sell imaginary ladders to people stuck in a hole, promising they'll climb out if they sell more imaginary ladders.

6   MLM: Multi-Level Marketing: The legal version—now with real ladders sold to people who don't need them yet. But trust me, they'll find themselves in a hole soon.

Aadi was undeterred—because why would he ever be deterred by something as trivial as logic?

He conjured a glowing ball. It buzzed, it pulsed… and you just knew it wasn't going to last.

Ityadi carefully observed the orb. For once, she found it beautiful. Then she quickly realized that the department of appreciating beauty wasn't hers.

"That doesn't look stable," Ityadi observed.

"It's not supposed to be stable!" Aadi shot back, glowing defiantly. "Chaos is the secret ingredient. That's where the magic happens."

That's also where lawsuits happen… but let's not get ahead of ourselves.

Chintu 2.0 was damned from the start—a sequel with a bigger budget but the same doomed script.

Ityadi leaned closer, her silver glow sharpening. "You know, Aadi, if you want a *flawless* network, make it hierarchical. You do love being on top, don't you?"

She left the rest unsaid, but Aadi's glow turned a slightly rosy hue.

"Hierarchical! Yes! That's genius, Ityadi!"

Aadi lifted the orb dramatically. "Behold! The moment that will create eternity!"

And without so much as a second thought—or even a first one—he released it.

The orb blew.

Not the dignified, cinematic kind.

More like someone lit fireworks in a public toilet—messy, loud, and full of flying bits you'd rather not think about.

Did the particles know what they were doing? *Nope.*

Did they care? *Also nope.*

But they sure looked like they were having the time of their lives.

"A masterpiece of creation!" Aadi declared, basking in his own brilliance.

Ityadi shook her head. "Looks more like an unlicensed daycare."

Patterns began to form. Forces settled down, pulling particles into fragile structures.

Stars flared up.

They were practically yelling, *"I'm the center of the universe!"* Typical—give something a little energy, and suddenly it's a diva.

`#BurnBrightDieYoung` feels like the universe's first trending hashtag, courtesy of its original influencers.

Galaxies emerged, each one convinced it was the best thing to happen since hydrogen.

Some galaxies whined like the bridegroom's drunk *Fuffadji*[7] at a Punjabi wedding—loud, persistent, and determined to ruin everything and everyone in each frame they appeared in.

Some of them were the irregular galaxies.

Cosmic LOLs of stars.

Unapologetically themselves, dancing barefoot at a black-tie event.

Amid all the cosmic chaos, these *malangs* were kind of beautiful—just here for a good time, not a long time.

Aadi and Ityadi dismissed them, of course.

The irregular galaxies, apparently, weren't worth their bandwidth. They were too weird, too unpredictable.

---

7   My editor suggested replacing "bridegroom's Fuffadji at a Punjabi wedding" with a different analogy for global appeal.
I suggested they actually meet one to truly understand Fuffad-ism. The compromise? This footnote. Now, the global audience can enjoy another quirk.

The best things in creation often go unnoticed by those too busy admiring their own reflection.

Black holes prowled the cosmos, swallowing anything they pleased. Less black holes, more creation's assholes.

They'd snatch your lunch, then eat your Tupperware for good measure. And they'd still blame you for bringing it anywhere near them.

"Nice galaxy," one black hole presumably purred. "Shame if someone… made it a snack."

Nom. Nom. Nom.

Frankly, I'd seen enough.

Time to fast-forward a few billion years (in your timeline, that is). Because who really wants to watch cosmic puberty unfold in real time?

If you are still interested in the teenage acne revelations of the cosmos, bookmark this page, watch National Geographic for a bit and then come back.

Among all the spinning planets and drifting debris, one caught Aadi's eye.

By cosmic standards, it was laughably unremarkable—a small, fragile planet, wobbling its way around a third-rate star.

But Aadi was captivated.

"Look at it," he said, his glow softening. "A delicate little jewel spinning like it's got something to prove."

Ityadi squinted like a jeweler inspecting a cracked cubic zirconia. "It's lopsided, unstable, and barely holding together. Your taste is as bad as your project management skills."

"It's the edge of ruin that creates brilliance," Aadi murmured. "Fragility... that's where the magic is."

Sure. Very Instagrammable quote, Aadi.

But hey, who am I to ruin the moment for Chintu 2.1[8]?

The Void already grabbed a plate—buffet time!

---

8   Why not Chintu 3.0, you ask? Look, we live in a world where Firefox is at version 134.0.2. If humanity insists on that level of absurdity, at least the cosmos—where black holes eat stars—can show some restraint when it comes to major versioning. Though, given the universe and the Earth's place in it, it should probably be something like Chintu 2.0.0.0.1—and that's me being generous. But hey, I'm not the narrator up there.

The Lucky Loser

Alittle rock spun through cosmic chaos.
Scarred, battered, and somehow too dumb to die. Like a cosmic cockroach, clinging to chaos.

Stars exploded, galaxies collided—and through it all, it refused to quit.

Aadi noticed and drifted closer.

"It's perfect," he whispered, his glow trembling with childlike excitement. "It's ready. Not too hot, not too cold. Just right."

You'd think he was describing porridge. But no, he was talking about this rock.

"What's your genius plan this time?" Ityadi frowned. "Fireworks? Lava fountains? Or are we skipping the foreplay and jumping straight to the tragic finale?"

Aadi didn't answer.

He saw something in the rock that neither Ityadi nor I could fathom—potential, or maybe just another outlet for his relentless ambition.

His voice swelled with purpose.

"Let there be—"

"—mess?"

"Life."

Little did I know, this moment would give birth to bad choreography.

Deep within the rock's oceans, molecules began their chaotic dance.

Cells split, merged, and re-split in an endless loop of trial and error.

Creation hurled dirty socks at the cosmic wall, hoping something—*anything filthy enough*—would cling for dear life.

It was life's very first attempt, and it showed.

"They're multiplying!" Aadi marveled, his voice tinged with awe, like he'd just discovered *curcumin latte*[9].

If he threw out one more exclamation point, it was going to smack me right between the eyes. I had bigger problems with his punctuation than with his enthusiasm.

---

9   Curcumin Latte: A beverage that takes grandma's no-nonsense home remedy, slaps a $6 price tag on it, and serves it in a cup that disintegrates before you finish. If you actually want the benefits instead of just an Instagram post, toss some turmeric in a spoon of hot *ghee*, stir it into hot milk, and drink it like an adult.

"Bravo," said Ityadi, a study in monotone. She wasn't interested anymore.

Aadi ignored her entirely.

For him, this was greatness unfolding—too profound for Ityadi's cynical mind to appreciate.

The cells began to specialize, each one declaring itself superior to the last.

Some became fish.

Before me swam the beta version of *Bangalore*[10] during rush hour. Prehistoric fish zigzagged in chaotic patterns, honking silently at each other as if yelling, *"Swim faster, da[11]!"*

For all the chaos, there was something undeniably poetic about it.

Some fish grew legs and got adventurous. They flopped onto land.

Legs? *Check*.

Lungs? *Oops*.

They wheezed like gym newbies on a treadmill but stubbornly kept going.

Sometimes in life, by the time you learn the truth, you're either too late... *or too dead*.

"They're learning to—"

"—be on someone's lunch menu."

Aadi hovered over a struggling one with irritation. "Why are you so slow? Move. Evolve already! Do I have to do everything myself?"

---

10 Bangalore: A globally renowned name for Bengaluru, an Indian city famous for its weather—and for the software industry which ruined it.

11 da: A tiny word with a huge split personality disorder. Depending on Bengaluru's weather, it could mean anything from 'bro' to 'dude' to 'you idiot'.

Pro tip: Yelling at evolution doesn't turn it into same-day shipping—but try telling Aadi that.

Eventually, one fish made it. It flopped onto the land, barely alive, but triumphant.

"See? *Aadi fish*. First of its name."

Evolution raced forward in Aadi's mind like a YouTube video on 100x speed. For everything else, it was buffering.

Aadi wasn't in the mood to stop now.

He had already invented the *"Let there be [insert whatever]!"* parameterized template for creation.

"Let there be dinosaurs!" Aadi announced.

"Let there be giant reptiles with pea-sized brains," Ityadi muttered. Her quips were slowing now, her fatigue beginning to show.

Aadi didn't notice. His attention was fully consumed by his new masterpieces.

Dinosaurs stomped across the land like kids on a Red Bull binge, their massive frames crashing through anything in their path.

One particularly enthusiastic specimen spun in hopeless circles, chasing its tail.

Another hurled its head into a tree trunk with such conviction, I almost respected it.

But here's the thing about dinosaurs: no matter how much stomping they did, they remained at the mercy of the universe.

High overhead, a fiery streak tore through the sky, growing brighter by the second.

The meteor was not just falling—it was gunning for the planet with the unstoppable force of a late delivery truck.

Ityadi tilted toward it, her silver light dimming. "Aadi, I really think you should—"

"Focus," he snapped, hugging the planet in a tyrannical glow, as if sheer arrogance could scare the meteor into turning around.

Ityadi leaned back, her sharpness surprisingly muted. "Aadi, this is—"

"I said *focus*. Don't distract me," he hissed, doubling down on the drama.

The meteor—a molten missile of doom—kept coming, utterly disinterested in Aadi's monologue.

"Aadi, stop," Ityadi tried again, her voice going soft. "You'll lose everything you've built."

"I won't." His glow flared defiantly.

But meteors don't have a *Stop* button.

With a cosmic *I told you so*—the universe's version of a long-overdue punchline—it slammed into the planet.

The planet shuddered. Continents cracked like dropped plates, and the air itself turned to fire.

Just like that, the dinosaurs were gone.

Sorry, T-Rex, your meteor insurance didn't cover extinction.

Ityadi watched the fallout with quiet resignation.

She had seen this pattern play out before: creation, destruction, and the relentless arrogance of a creator who thought he could outwit chaos.

"This should be it," she thought, watching the dinosaurs vanish. "With them gone…"

I thought so, too.

The Void burped.

Life refused to quit.

It reshaped itself, donned chaos like a dented battle suit, and dared extinction to try again.

Life is stubborn like that—a toddler headbutting a table, convinced it can intimidate physics.

Let's not get carried away.

The book has only so many pages, and you have only so much patience.

It's better to move along before evolution cracks the chicken-and-egg paradox. Some mysteries deserve their privacy.

Don't worry.

I won't drag you through the slow grind of survival.

It's way more fun when evolution starts showing off.

From the ashes, life spat out something new: *monkeys*.

Smart enough to be dangerous and dumb enough to make you worry.

"Do you see that?" Aadi asked softly, not with doubt but something heavier.

Determination? Fear? Or the unbearable weight of a dream he couldn't let go of?

"Hmm…" That's all Ityadi muttered. At this point, her interest was thinner than a budget airline seat cushion.

Aadi didn't wait. Now, he rarely did.

He drifted closer to the monkeys. There was something about them—something different—that he saw.

"This," he whispered to no one in particular, "is what I've been waiting for."

All I could see was the *Cosmic 3C*[12].

Creation. Critique. Chaos.

One monkey used the stick to prod another, as if testing the limits of friendship… or patience.

---

12   3C: Not to be confused with the Agile world's 3C, though arguably even that has cosmic origins—if you take the background picture on the Agile manifesto website seriously.

Another hurled a rock straight at its own foot, squawking indignantly at the pain, as if the betrayal had come from the rock itself.

A third climbed a tree, forgot *why*, and promptly fell onto a group below. Monkeys did what monkeys do. His banana? Collateral damage.

High above, an older monkey scratched its head, surveying the chaos with a look that said, *Fools. All of them. Bananas demand respect.*

"Yes! This is it," Aadi proclaimed, pointing at a monkey gnawing its own foot. "From these fools will rise the ones who will craft monuments in my name. My legacy begins *here*."

Aadi's grand plan rested on these chaotic fools.

Because clearly, the road to legacy begins with a species that can't even handle a banana.

Sometimes, ambition is like a bad poker hand—the more you pour in, the harder it gets to admit you're losing.

Aadi wasn't about to fold.

"Aadi, can't you see?" Ityadi intervened, her tone unusually gentle. "You're giving everything to this... and when it breaks, who's going to hold you together?"

"You're wrong," he snapped. "Always wrong. Always jealous."

"Then maybe you don't need me anymore." Her glow lingered for a moment, dim and uncertain, as if waiting for Aadi to speak.

Aadi didn't say anything.

He didn't look at her.

He didn't even turn to watch her go.

"This is the beginning," Aadi whispered.

It always *is*—the beginning of something, the end of something else, and the middle of a mess.

As Ityadi faded into the Void, my attention shifted to the creatures below. I was worried about these new evolved beings.

Their talent for imitation unnerved me, especially the thought of them imitating Aadi in their evolution.

Without Ityadi, this development horrified me.

I didn't yet realize how much I had to fear.

The rock, blissfully unaware that it had just won the cosmic lottery, spun on.

This lucky loser had no idea it wasn't supposed to make it this far. Its survival wasn't brilliance or design—just dumb, blind luck.

It was hurled into the spotlight, courtesy of a creator mesmerized by the endless temptation of *What if.*

Above, another meteor blazed, its trajectory uncertain but its challenge unmistakable.

It hung there—watching, waiting—as if daring Aadi to rewrite destiny once more.

It's a quiet reminder that even dumb luck runs out eventually. And when it does, it's usually spectacular.

The Offense Cortex

Once, they swung from trees, flung fruit, and lived blissfully unaware of their cosmic insignificance.

They didn't question their place in the cosmos—or why bananas seemed to shrink every year.

Then Aadi, drunk on ambition, decided it was time for upgrades.

Fire.

Bigger brains.

And the worst of them all—a permanent headache called *self-importance*.

Giving advanced tools to creatures who mistook sticks for snakes and snakes for gods? Cosmic comedy gold.

"You're special," Aadi told them.

They believed him—mistake number one.

Worse, *he* believed it too—mistake number two.

Cavemen swapped branches for clubs, discovered fire, and began grunting in full sentences.

"Language!" Aadi declared proudly. "My ultimate masterpiece."

Ityadi, watching from the Void, merely raised an eyebrow but stayed silent.

Meanwhile, down below, a tribe gathered around a fire.

Bruk, chest puffed out, declared, "Me kill mammoth!"

Mammoth kills were rare—this should've earned him instant respect.

But Zug, arms crossed, wasn't buying it.

"Me see mammoth by river. Mammoth alive."

And just like that, the vibe shifted from awe to *Hang on a minute, Bruk.*

Bruk hesitated, then blurted, "Not same mammoth. That mammoth cousin. Me kill original."

Zug snorted. "No blood. No tracks. You lie."

"Not lie!" Bruk roared. "Alternative truth!" he barked, pioneering the fine art of absolute nonsense.

The tribe didn't have a word for *propaganda* yet—but give them time. Humans always invent words for their worst habits.

Above, Aadi groaned. "Lying? Already? That wasn't supposed to start for centuries."

Ityadi's silence spoke volumes.

Grunts turned into arguments. Sticks became weapons. And weapons? They evolved into humanity's most devastating invention: *weaponized thought*.

And so, humans staggered into what would later be glorified as *civilization*—a peculiar experiment where lies grew fatter, weapons got deadlier and bananas... well, they're still shrinking.

One day, Aadi caught a hint of something lurking deep in human minds.

"Who are you?" he demanded.

The thing smirked. "Name's Cortex. Offense Cortex. You made me, boss."

"No, I didn't."

"Oh, but you did. You gave them brains, didn't you? And here I am." It leaned closer, whispering, "By the way, that funny bone you planted to help them laugh things off? Gone. Extinct."

Aadi blinked. "Why didn't I notice you earlier?"

The Cortex grinned. "You didn't stop at brains, boss. You thought bigger brains would mean bigger ideas—but they went for bigger sting."

"What sting?" Aadi asked, already regretting it.

"An extra brain chunk, boss. Slipped in right below the backbone, where irritation thrives. I'm rooted so deep, they've to self-poke halfway to their appendix to tickle me. And, they love it. Oh, they can't stop. And me? *Mmmmm...* I relish it." the Cortex chimed.

Aadi cringed. "You mean, in their—?"

Dear reader, this is where divine decorum kicks in—but you get the idea.

Before Aadi could protest, the Cortex dove into human minds and... well, *wherever else*, for their poking pleasures.

At first, the Cortex's work was crude.

One day, Zug stumbled into the cave, blood dripping down his face. He clutched his head, eyes darting wildly.

"Who hit Zug?" he growled, his voice low, dripping with suspicion.

Bruk stepped forward. "Zug fall? Cliff slippery."

Zug shook his head, wincing. "No fall. Someone hit. While sleep." He pointed to his head, "Blood proof!" As if logic had ever solved anything.

A tense hush fell over the cave.

Zug glared at Bruk. "Yesterday, me insult Bruk's mammoth painting. Say look like goat. Bruk mad?"

Bruk clutched his club behind his back. "Bruk peaceful," he said, too quickly. "But mammoth painting… mammoth painting offended."

All eyes turned to the crude mess of scratches on the cave wall. The mammoth painting loomed over them like a prehistoric meme, gone viral for all the wrong reasons.

"Mammoth sacred!" Bruk declared, bowing dramatically to the painting.

The others hesitated, then followed suit, nervously chanting nonsense syllables—as if their devotion might save them from the divine mammoth's wrath.

Zug, his suspicion momentarily forgotten, rubbed his bloody head against the painting. Maybe for forgiveness. Maybe for favor. Maybe because brains don't work after head hit.

Aadi pointed proudly at the bustling civilization below.

"There, near the Indus. They've built cities, mastered philosophy, and invented zero. Isn't it magnificent?"

The Offense Cortex groaned, stretching its ethereal tendrils. "Yeah, yeah, they're great. But do you have *any* idea how exhausting it is to keep this many people offended 24/7?"

Aadi was amused. "You seem... tired. Why?"

The Cortex waved dramatically toward the ground. "Because they're too good at guilt! I tried to start a harmless family feud over a missed *yajna*[13] invitation. Next thing I know, the brother is crying about his *karma*[14], and writing entire texts about how unworthy he is. I meant just a little offense. They're ruining my work!"

Aadi laughed. "So, they've... out-offended you?"

"Precisely!" the Cortex huffed. "He went off to meditate, came back enlightened, and started a new school of thought on forgiveness. *Forgiveness!* Ugh, it's exhausting. How am I supposed to do my job when they keep turning offenses into philosophical breakthroughs?"

The Cortex needed a strategy—something cunning, something with numbers.

And thus, the pinnacle of deceit was born: *statistics*.

It quickly curated a special subset of humans who thrived on being offended.

These humans found strange pleasure in getting upset, poking a hidden nerve they simply couldn't resist.

---

13   Yajna: A sacred ritual involving offerings to the divine, traditionally performed with utmost reverence, precision, and a remarkably low tolerance for guest list errors. Forget to invite someone? It's the ancient equivalent of unfriending them on every celestial platform.

14   Karma: The cosmic ledger that meticulously tracks your deeds, misdeeds—and whether you left the bathroom light on.

Indignation became an addiction—more potent than joy, more seductive than laughter.

Tribes became towns, towns became empires. But the funny bone? That became a fossil.

Disagreements turned into wars over who owned the truth. Socrates drank his hemlock not for questioning gods but for questioning egos.

Ideas became prey, hunted like prehistoric beasts.

The Cortex perched smugly on Aadi's shoulder. "Efficient, isn't it? No spears. Just words sharp enough to gut each other."

Aadi watched in silence. Below, a young astronomer sketched the stars, blissfully oblivious to the brewing storm.

"Galileo," Aadi sighed. "You're next."

In the chambers of the Inquisition, the Cortex rested on a shelf, invisible but buzzing with energy.

"He claims Earth isn't the center of the universe," it whispered to a cardinal. "So... does that make *you* irrelevant?" It twisted the knife.

The murmurs grew louder until a voice thundered, "Heresy!"

Galileo, standing alone, sighed and pointed at his telescope. "It's right there. See for yourself."

The Cortex yawned. *Or don't. Why let facts ruin the pleasure of perfect outrage?*

Then it teased another one, "He called your mother Earth a liar. Don't know about you. But the place where I come from, we take our mammas very seriously."

Poor Galileo—a warning for the future thinkers, etched in history.

"Is this why I gave you brains, you idiots!" Aadi shouted.

But this was still just the beginning.

Over centuries, the Cortex refined its arsenal.

Cancel culture? The Cortex didn't invent the concept—it just turned up the speed. It turned mosquito bites into full-blown moral crises.

Darwin studied evolution but missed the Cortex.

Survival of the fittest?

No.

Survival of the whiniest—those who mastered the art of shouting the loudest.

Aadi gave humans great gifts: empires, faiths, political systems.

They twisted these gifts into untouchable truths, guarding their beliefs like jealous dragons hoarding treasure.

Once, the Earth itself spun backward for ten minutes in a cosmic hiccup, as if to say, "Are you sure about all this?"

Humans didn't notice. Too busy arguing.

Disgruntled by it all, Aadi threw in famines, plagues, volcanic eruptions, floods …. chaos upon chaos.

And no one ever whispered, "*Aadi, you've gone too far.*"

Frustrated with the human evolution, Aadi shaped a mimicry of Ityadi, hoping it would cut through the Void.

The flickering echo that emerged was hollow, lifeless—much like humanity's humor, drained of its sting.

"How am I doing?" Aadi asked.

"Good effort," it replied, its voice flat and mechanical.

Aadi stared at it, waiting for the sharp wit and brutal honesty that always accompanied Ityadi's presence.

Nothing came. No barbed observation. No dismantling of his ego.

This thing? This echo? It was useless—a hollow mockery of the voice he feared and needed.

"You're no critic," he spat, smashing it to pieces.

The shards scattered across the Void, glinting like a thousand voiceless stars.

For the first time, Aadi truly felt alone.

He turned his gaze back to Earth.

"At least these *morons* still surprise me."

By the modern age, the Cortex was fully grown.

No need for real grievances.

Someone tripped over a sidewalk, and ten million people demanded the sidewalk be fired.

A stray typo, a hashtag, an emoji in the wrong context.

Offense didn't need logic, just opportunity.

Even knock-knock jokes came with disclaimers: *'No doors were offended in the making of this joke'.*

`#Sarcasm` ruined sarcasm itself, killing even the slightest hint of irony. Hashtags buried humor under a tombstone that read, "This is not a tombstone."

"Mistake number three," Aadi sighed. "Thinking they'd ever learn."

"Perfect!" the Cortex hissed. "You used to throw plagues, boss. I just give them trending topics."

Aadi glanced at Ityadi's empty seat.

A silent reminder of what he had lost. Once, she would've been there, challenging him, stripping him bare with her critiques.

Too proud, she would've said. *Vision of a god, judgment of a child.*

But she was gone.

"At least argue with me, dammit." His voice echoed into the Void.

No response.

"You were right," he whispered, his words barely audible. "You always were."

As Aadi faded into the Void, his glow flickered, a dim ember against the vast darkness.

He looked down one last time at humans warring over rumors.

#WhereIsHe, one side raged.

#WeNeedNoCreator, the other retorted.

"I offered them the stars," Aadi muttered, his voice heavy with regret, "but they turned their gaze to each other, finding only shadows."

His light dimmed further. "They've already set everything ablaze. Let them burn."

"If you insist, boss," the Cortex sneered, its tendrils curling smugly as it struck the match.

The Rejects

Consider this ant.

Just minding its own business, dragging crumbs back to the colony like the tiny blue-collar worker it is.

Then one day, it sees its shadow—a big, towering thing stretching out like it's the king of the jungle.

And this ant? It's hooked. Starts thinking, *Oh, that's the real me. Look at how massive I am!*

So now, this little idiot starts strutting around, chasing the perfect light. It skips work, basking in the sun like it's God's gift to insects.

Then noon hits. The shadow? Gone. *Poof.*

Now the ant's standing there, staring at the ground, utterly confused, like, *Wait, did my greatness just take a lunch break?*

Look, you're just an ant.

You never were the shadow.

You're five millimeters tall—tops.

Get over yourself.

1979. VisiCalc, the first spreadsheet, unknowingly laid the foundation of modern testing: copy, paste, and pray.

But this story is *not* about VisiCalc.

It's about Mel Brooks[15].

---

15 Mel Brooks: Don't know him? Pause, Google, and thank me later. Creator of History of the World, Part I and a thousand other comedic masterpieces. Knowing him will make this chapter hit harder. Trust me.

A historian and accidental revolutionary, he walked into the caves with purpose.

Tomorrow, the world would disown him. Today, he didn't care.

History loves to yank brilliant minds off their pedestals. Brooks is a modern Galileo—minus the telescope, plus a flair for absurdity.

He wasn't looking for glory.

He was looking for a story.

Naturally, *glory* found him first.

The caves were full of scratched walls and stick figures.

Dismissed by experts as the prehistoric version of public restroom graffiti—an anthropological term for *meh*.

Brooks wasn't buying it.

He studied the carvings, tracing them with his fingers.

Something about the scratches felt deliberate. They weren't just random scrawls of a bored caveman, but purposeful, as if left for someone to find.

One showed a figure mid-stream, marking his dominance in the most primal way.

"It's as if someone knew I'd be standing here," Brooks muttered to himself—the thought was ridiculous, but it refused to let go.

Brooks grinned, the kind of grin only a man who doesn't realize he's shaping history can muster.

"Anyone else see it?" Brooks asked.

"See what?"

"That one's either creating modern art or proving Darwin wrong or just taking a leak on someone's rabbit art. Honestly, could be all three."

Where others saw meaningless scratches, Brooks saw a trifecta of cultural achievement etched in stone.

After the revelation, Brooks did what historians do.

He wrote it down:

Creation is chaos.

Someone yelling, 'Are you sure?', turns it into art.

To Brooks, the figure mid-stream wasn't just relieving himself—he was critiquing.

A prehistoric jester, standing defiantly in the margins of history, mocking the earnest hunter's attempt at art.

Cavemen had jesters, Brooks decided.

Every tribe needed someone to remind the hunters and artists not to take themselves *too* seriously.

Someone to keep egos in check, to poke fun at the sanctity of the moment.

Someone to question, challenge, and provoke.

"Where are our jesters—the testers? The ones brave enough to laugh at broken things before they become sacred?" Brooks laughed to himself, pen scratching against paper. "Maybe we lost something when we stopped making room for the *pee-in-the-corner* guy," he wrote. "Maybe he was the only one truly paying attention."

For two years, he wrote on the origins of critique, unaware that he was rewriting its future.

These murals were no accident.

They were the last footprints of Ityadi, carefully planted for exactly Brooks—and Brooks alone.

He thought he was just a passerby in history, a curious observer.

Little did he know that he was Ityadi's handpicked pawn in an eternal dance between creation and critique—Aadi and Ityadi, two forces much, much older than the first scratch on the cave wall.

Brooks, the accidental prophet, I chuckled.

You can't make this stuff up.

History of the World Part I hit theaters in 1981.

Brooks put his two years of research to work, showcasing the world's first critic.

A pissing caveman, pissing off everyone around him.

Developers, the modern Aadis of their digital universes, watched, nodded, and returned to their keyboards.

They acted like gods because they could type curly braces—still certain they could simply test their own code.

You know, like sniffing milk to see if it's gone bad, then drinking it anyway.

Guesswork posing as diligence.

For the Rejects though, it wasn't just a film. It was their chance to matter.

They were the exiles from the promised land of creation: too logical for marketing, too skeptical for development.

The Rejects found salvation in critique. They decided their existence had only one purpose—ruining illusions.

If developers were Aadis, the Rejects were shadows of Ityadi, whispering, *Try again*.

Unsung heroes? More like unsung hooligans.

Brooks was only documenting history.

But since when have revolutions cared about intent? They just need two things: a slogan and a basement.

The Rejects already had the basement—a dark, damp, and pungent space, perfect for conspiratorial zeal.

Now they just needed a slogan catchy enough to slap on T-shirts.

"Question everything!" someone shouted.

"Too generic!" another barked.

"What about *No Bug Left Behind*?"

A murmur of approval rippled through the room… and then died.

"Sounds like a charity for cockroaches," someone objected.

"Critique Happens!" another voice called.

The room paused. It was awful. It was genius.

Absolutely perfect for a coffee mug.

"Let's put that in Comic Sans[16]," someone quipped.

"It's a crime against fonts," another retorted.

"Or… is it so bad it's revolutionary?"

---

16 Comic Sans is the font that packs up for the circus but accidentally shows up at a corporate meeting. It's the font that forgot to read the room—much like half the jokes in this book. Fun for three minutes, until everyone's begging for Times New Roman to teach decades-old test techniques again.

The room fell silent. For the first time, the Rejects agreed—it was both.

In their zeal to mock everything, they forgot: critique wasn't meant to entertain, it was meant to matter.

They didn't agree on much, but they all knew one thing: they had nothing to lose.

That made them dangerous—or just loud.

Very, very loud.

Testers. That's what the Rejects called themselves now.

By the time the testers hit the mainstream, critique was less about revelation and more about who could shout *"This sucks!"* the loudest.

The IT world caught on.

Testing wasn't a task or a side gig anymore—it became a full-fledged role.

Grudgingly, companies began hiring testers as critics with business cards. They even built processes around critique.

Developers tolerated testers the way cats tolerate humans. With an air of superiority, and an unshakable belief that they'd do just fine without them.

The reluctant acceptance of testing evolved into a full-blown industry—complete with certifications, conferences, and an inexplicable obsession with swag bags.

Then testers crossed the ultimate line: they started handing out awards to themselves.

Awards! Developers completely lost it.

A public event shattered the delicate balance between developers and testers, once and for all.

At a packed conference, amid the glow of PowerPoint slides and free donuts, a tester declared, "Without us, the code would collapse!"

From the back, a developer muttered, "Without us, there'd be no code to collapse."

"Without us, you'd be debugging this bug's grandkids until your funeral."

"Without us, you'd be unemployed."

Without both of you, humanity would still be the same shit.

Developers saw testers as parasites, sucking the life out of their creativity.

Testers saw developers as bacteria: chaotic, stubborn, and impossible to contain.

I thought how lame they both were. Parasites? Bacteria? These amateurs couldn't even insult each other properly.

They fought over testing like ants debating the strategic merit of carrying one crumb or two.

Fascinating to them, exhausting to everyone else.

Brooks eventually learned that he was being hailed as the *Father of Testing*.

He was startled—and cracked a bastard joke that could get this book banned.

So, let's stick with the other thing he said.

"They started a movement?" he laughed. "Good for them. I just wanted to make cavemen look ridiculous."

One minute he's making dick jokes in togas, the next he's the patron saint of software testing.

What a world.

The ant was probably right. Shadows can outperform and outlive those who cast them.

Just ask Mel Brooks.

The Backup Plan

The Brooks revolution turned the world into a dumpster fire.

Years crawled by, each one piling on fresh chaos like kindling to the blaze.

Developers ran wild, drunk on their unchecked ideas and completely unstoppable—breaking things so fast that even their bug trackers begged for mercy.

Testers didn't clean up. They flagged the mess with smug smiles, mixing alchemy with wishful thinking. Worse, they automated their own stupidity, slapped on an 'AI-powered' label, and called it progress.

The industry didn't need heroes. It needed metrics that fed vanity instead of critique.

Beautiful yet meaningless graphs that whispered, *You're doing great, sweetie.*

Humanity had a grand tool for self-awareness: **critique**. Yet they wielded it with all the grace of a chimp juggling scissors.

Every time they bled, they blamed the scissors for not being idiot-proof.

Critique didn't disappear—it was betrayed.

No longer a force that shaped brilliance.

It became a cheap trinket, sold by the pound to anyone with a budget to burn.

Packaged, priced, and peddled by testers who didn't understand it, sold to developers who didn't want it, and ignored by consumers who didn't care.

"What a disaster!"

The sudden proclamation caught me off guard.

The voice was sharp—like an unexpected ice shard in a warm drink. ***Ityadi!***

She emerged from the Void. Her silvery aura cutting sharper than before, as if the Void itself had tempered her edges.

"The Brooks Revolution has failed," she declared, her voice a blade. "Look at them... these fools. Critique was never meant to be a garnish for creation. It's the knife that carves it into something worth keeping."

I said nothing. I'm not supposed to speak. Observing is my role.

That—and not getting on Ityadi's bad side. A survival instinct I'm quite proud of.

"Promise me something?" she said, her tone softer now.

Dangerous.

A promise requiring near-infinite suspension of disbelief?

Sure. That's how cosmic bargains always start.

I gulped. "Uh… okay?"

Ityadi pointed to a human.

"Him?" I asked. "The last potato in the pantry?"

"Yes, I've searched far and wide for a worthy author. I found a few… too busy pitching their own agendas." Ityadi said with a sharp edge. "This is the backup plan."

"Twenty years and still a tester," I muttered.

"I know."

"He has a… reputation."

"I know."

"Annoying. Overly opinionated. Offended half the industry, if not more."

"…"

"Probably forgot if he locked the front door this morning," I offered as a last resort.

"Well, he's breathing, isn't he?" she sighed.

Breathing? That's the bar now?

Ityadi turned back to the Void, her glow softening.

For a moment, I saw doubt flickering in her eyes.

"He'll do," she said. "He has to."

Great choice, Ityadi—truly inspiring.

It wasn't a Plan B.

It was a Plan Z with no contingencies.

Rahul Verma[17] was born in a sleepy Indian town in 1981, his arrival accompanied by a cosmic shrug.

---

17 Rahul Verma: Yours Truly. If you are paying attention, I'm the author of this exceptionally well-written paperweight.

The place was so quiet that his newborn snores were mistaken for the monsoon forecast—slightly more accurate than DD1's[18] weather report.

From day one, it was obvious: greatness wouldn't be calling.

But luck?

Luck had him on speed dial.

Luck trailed him like a faithful dog, wagging its tail wherever he went.

His toilet paper scribbles were hailed as profound insights, leading to conference invites, keynote slots, and at least one honorary mug.

Ityadi's the most meticulous being I have seen. Her decisions were always deliberate, as unyielding as the tick of time.

Rahul in her cosmic plan felt like she'd thrown a dart blindfolded—using the wrong end of the dart.

Did she see something I didn't?

What if she didn't want me to see what she saw?

What if the flaws I saw were exactly what her plan needed?

The thoughts made my stomach churn. There was an unease I couldn't pinpoint.

My gut urged me to voice my concerns, but I was too busy trying to please her.

What a fool I was.

I started with the nudges, quiet whispers.

I shadowed Rahul through every step of his life.

I started small, scattering hints of a greater purpose just out of reach.

---

18 DD1: One of India's two state-owned channels at the time. It made epics on a budget so tight, the cast had to bring their own lunch— and that lunch still had more plot than some modern blockbusters.

A tea stain shaped like a question mark.
A mirror whispering riddles in his dreams.
Subtlety wasn't working.
Divine intervention was hitting voicemail.
I left so many signs, I was half convinced he'd try unsubscribing from the Universe.
To hell with whispers—*it's time to shake the cat.*

Rahul was sprawled across his bed like a half-asleep human Garfield, drool pooling on his pillow.

I slipped into his dream, braced for confusion—and, naturally found myself drowning in it. He groaned, rolled over, and muttered "Chah!" (Tea).

Rahul had never faced truth and I am Satyadi, the Truth personified.

When I dictated the book, he grabbed a pen. Or so he thought. It was the TV remote. A promising start.

His first attempt at writing wasn't sentences, it was hieroglyphics. They were crime scenes in ink.

Rahul's greatest achievement wasn't finishing the book— it was convincing himself he deserved to write it.

This guy? This is who Ityadi chose?
Desperate times call for questionable choices.

And so, *The Last Book on Testing* was born.

A final critique scrawled in the margins of eternity.

A cautionary pamphlet for whatever comes next.

This book as it stands—though dictated by me—is at the mercy of Rahul.

His sarcasm concerns me, but I think there are human limits to how many jokes one can cram onto a page.

He's human, after all. Well... *almost.*

I trust this book reaches you mostly in the serious tone in which I dictated it—if not entirely.

Knowing Rahul, he probably slipped in a pun or three when I wasn't looking. But in a 10,000-page book[19], that's hardly a concern for either of us.

I am not found in creation's brilliance or critique's sharpness. Those are the domains of Aadi and Ityadi.

I reside in the absurd gamble that someone—anyone—can fix what the cosmos has broken.

Hope just asks for someone foolish enough to try and too stubborn to quit.

Rahul wasn't chosen for being extraordinary. He was chosen precisely because he wasn't.

Systems don't thrive *in spite* of average people.

They thrive *because* of them.

---

19 I'll cover the other 9,750 pages in The Second Last Book on Testing. Hang on—doesn't that make this one The Third Last Book on Testing? Never mind. ISBN's locked in, and let's be honest, a change in title wouldn't make you pay more for the book.

The Breadcrumbs

et's take a moment.
You've survived *Aadhār Khand*. That's no small feat.

You've outlasted cosmic tantrums, existential ramblings, and at least two jokes that should've been cut.

Celebrate—but remember: survival isn't victory, it's just the prelude to round two.

This was the trailer. The real drama begins now.

By now, it's clear this book isn't for PowerPoint ninjas or LinkedIn hustlers.

It's not for those who believe they've patented critical thinking or that their hashtags disrupted enlightenment.

It's for those who still find wisdom in questions and solace in a good laugh

This is a book for seekers, not preachers.

The cosmos is gloriously ridiculous.

Reliving its absurdity while dictating this book to Rahul left me baffled—so baffled, in fact, that the only way to cope was by not taking myself seriously.

Neither should you.

Testing is divine comedy.

You poke holes in someone's masterpiece, critique it like a smug art critic who skipped art school, and still get paid for the privilege.

If that doesn't make you laugh, check your funny bone—it might need debugging. Tickle it while you still can.

Humor might be the last patch this world gets before the system crashes entirely.

There are no final answers.

Answers are stepping stones, not finish lines. They are just commas in sentences the universe hasn't finished writing yet.

The more you cling to them, the more they freeze your curiosity, boxing you into a smaller version of the infinite.

Test, probe, doubt, laugh, fail, retry, and rise again. That's what Ityadi tried to teach, what Aadi never understood, and what Rahul only pretended to grasp.

Ask questions—even the wrong ones. *Especially* the wrong ones.

Let the universe groan under the weight of your curiosity. If it drops a hint, grab it. Then drop that hint too.

Hints are hot potatoes.
Toss them fast, or risk getting burned.

This is your show now.
Let testing set you free. Feel confused—even silly.
Throw this book at a wall. Argue with it. Write angry notes in the margins. That's how you'll know it's working.
Just remember: a question answered too easily, probably was never answered at all.
Continue reading as a tester, as a seeker.

If you're still thinking, *What does this have to do with testing?*
That's adorable.
Keep asking questions like that, and one day, you might write a book nobody asked for—just like this one.
Now come on, fold this page into a paper plane and see how far confusion can fly.

Don't stop now.
Confusion is progress.
Humor is your cheat code.
Keep poking the universe until it laughs with you... or at you.
Every laugh, groan, or moment of WTF[20] is a breadcrumb leading you somewhere surprising.

---

20 WTF: Yeah, it means exactly what you think it does. Forget the PG nonsense—as if this book hasn't already offended some delicate sensibilities yet. WTF is a state of mind, a way to look at the universe and ask, *Really? What have you been smoking?* Honestly, it's the only feedback most books deserve... including this one.

२. AAKĀR KHAND

आकार खंड

The Circus

Delhi doesn't do subtle.
Neither in its slang nor its roasting.

Its ultimate roaster needs no shade, no shame, and no introductions. It's out there, naked, throwing SPF-defying punches: *the Delhi Sun.*

Delhi summers are not a season.

They are a test of human endurance, an annual championship where your will wrestles your sweat glands.

The air becomes your enemy and tempers hit their boiling point. Even the mangoes at the street stalls plead for early retirement in a fridge.

This story begins during one such summer, when even the shade couldn't keep its cool.

Shakuni Software[21].

Outside its office, electric wires tangled like the city's frayed nerves. Nearby, electric transformers hummed conspiratorially, as if exchanging classified intel about the heat.

Carts and cars joined in a chaotic symphony of yelling and honking—a soundtrack even chaos itself couldn't compose.

The air served an *all-you-can-breathe* buffet of dust and sweat, with suffocation served on the house.

As a finishing touch, the comforting smell of burning rubber wafted through.

Fresh air? Adorable. Delhi doesn't do that.

Joy shoved through the revolving doors, peeling himself out of Delhi's sweltering grip.

Forget bullet trains—Shakuni Software's entrance was a one-step portal from Delhi's inferno to Switzerland's icy calm.

The air-conditioning slapped him like a corporate dress code, whispering: *Behave.*

"*Namaste*[22], sir[23]," the guard said with practiced politeness.

---

21 Shakuni: In the Mahabharata, he plotted the downfall of dynasties—the OG mastermind of chaos, blending brilliance with moral bankruptcy. Coincidence? A reminder that bad decisions can be legendary. Just ask whoever named this place. Titanic Airways, anyone?

22 Namaste: The politest way to say, "I see you, I acknowledge you, and I absolutely do not want to shake hands."

23 Sir: Translates to 'Don't yell at me right now.'. 'Sir Sir Sir' means 'I'm listening.'. 'Sirji' indicates affection—and that you are not a Sir.

Jayakumar Natarajan nodded, unnoticeably. His friends call him *Joy*. We will too, for the sake of convenience.

The calm inside was a facade. Real chaos waited on the third floor. Up there, calm was just a rumor, and problems didn't walk—they sprinted.

The elevator dinged optimistically, as if it carried good news. It didn't. It was as trapped as everyone else inside.

Joy stepped in, catching his reflection in the brushed-metal doors.

Salt-and-pepper hair. Eyes permanently set to mid-sarcasm. The kind of face his team tolerated only because they had to.

"Who's doing what?" he muttered, a private ritual to distract himself from the grind.

Uma Roy, the Test Lead, juggling egos and deadlines for far too long.

Jasleen Kaur, the SDET—fierce with code but silent in meetings—a stark contrast to Kunal Joshi, the Ethical hacker whose T-shirts and playlist choices could spark HR hazards.

Yogendra Nath Dwivedi…, well Yogi was his favorite—less for his work and more for his poetic musings on the most mundane topics.

He would miss two of them:

Vikram Tanwar, the Test Manager, was on "personal leave"—a phrase that usually translated to wild conspiracy theories circulating through the office.

Debraj Gohain was in *Thailand* for a conference, because… of course, he was.

The elevator jolted to a stop, a harsh reminder that even machines hated Mondays.

He swiped his card at the entrance. A green light blinked, the turnstile clicked, and then came the pièce de résistance[24]: the attendance pen.

Why both systems? Redundancy? Mistrust? Or did someone think technology might call in sick? Joy often wondered.

Inside the department, the morning routine was already unfolding like a play too well-rehearsed.

Uma stood at her desk, muttering about "incomplete data." She looked up, meeting Joy's gaze. For a second, they shared the absurdity of it all. Then, she went back to work.

Jasleen sat at her desk, typing furiously, her monitor glowing like a spotlight on her grim focus. Joy avoided her eyebrows—*the bug fix she'd requested would have to wait.*

Humans excel at two things: creating problems and pretending they don't exist. At this moment, Joy embodied both.

Kunal lounged in his chair, nodding along to music only he could hear. His T-shirt declared: *"I May Be Wrong, But It's Highly Unlikely."* His fingers tapped lazily on the desk.

What music was he listening to, you ask? Curious cat, aren't you? Of course, I could tell you—but hasn't Kunal been stereotyped enough already?

Joy smirked, then slid into his chair.

The hum of his computer blended with the faint buzz of chatter. This chaos had an odd charm, one he couldn't quite explain.

Technically, he didn't need to be here. As the Development Lead, he could work from home. But the testers kept him coming back.

---

24 pièce de résistance: French for 'Look how cultured I am.' Just call it the 'centerpiece' like a normal person—unless you're some kind of onion-slicing maestro.

Not fondness, he thought. *That would be ridiculous. But something uncomfortably close to it.*

Joy couldn't name it, but I could see the feeling cling to him like secondhand smoke.

Some humans are drawn to places where failure and persistence share the same breath.

"Kunal, the reports," Uma said, her voice carrying a dangerously calm edge.

She rubbed her temples, the ghost of a headache already forming. Mondays were bad enough without having to chase Kunal for reports. Uma's frustration hung in the air like a storm cloud.

Joy figured this had to be her third—maybe fourth—attempt, half-expecting her to launch a stapler across the room. He silently prayed she'd aim well.

Kunal, blissfully lost in his music, didn't catch a word.

Joy called out, "Kunal!" loud enough to cut through the bass.

Kunal blinked, pulled out an earbud, and glanced over. "What?"

"Uma needs the reports," Joy said, suppressing a grin.

Kunal shrugged. "Chill, Uma. I don't need a babysitter," he muttered under his breath.

Before Uma could retaliate, Yogi strolled over, drying his hands on a paper towel. He had a knack for asking existential questions no one wanted answered. It was his gift—and the team's collective curse.

"*Arz kiya hai*[25]..." Yogi began, theatrically reciting Nida Fazli.

25 Arz Kiya Hai: Roughly translates to 'I present to you.' Traditionally used before a couplet, it's now co-opted by people who think they're the next Ghalib after two WhatsApp forwards.

"Munh ki baat sune har koyi,
dil ke dard ko jaane kaun?
Aawazon ke baazron mein,
khaamoshi pahchaane kaun?"

The world listens to spoken words
But who can grasp the heart's deep woe?
Amidst the clamor of endless chatter,
Who will hear silence echo?

Uma didn't miss a beat. "Kunal, obviously."

Joy hadn't expected the testing team to function so early.

Mornings usually began lazily, filled with gossip and half-hearted musings.

They cursed the coffee machine and waited for the vendor with freshly brewed tea, treating him like some sort of caffeine messiah.

Nobody was gossiping about Vikram, Joy thought—until Yogi dropped the catalyst. *Yogi, my boy,* he muttered under his breath.

"Where's Vikram sir?" Yogi asked, his timing as surgical as ever, shifting the room's energy with just one question.

"Hmm?" Uma barely looked up, too focused on her screen.

"Vikram. Where is he?" Yogi repeated, his voice dripping with faux innocence.

"Personal leave," Uma replied flatly.

Yogi's curiosity sharpened like a blade.

"*Driver's-license-renewal* leave, or *starting-a-goat-farm* leave?"

Joy smirked. "With Vikram, it could be either."

Jasleen chimed in, her voice calm but precise. "No 'synergy meeting' today."

Kunal erupted in loud laughter—a rare sound in the office. "So, let's fuck it up separately today."

Joy couldn't help but think: *Kunal has my vote for true synergy.*

Jasleen barely looked up from her screen. *"Oye!"* was the full extent of her disapproval.

Uma, sensing the team veering off course, intervened. "Enough. Let's get to work."

Jasleen's weaponized eyebrows eased into neutrality. *"Shukr hai."* (Thank God)

For a moment, the team felt oddly human—the grind paused for small, ridiculous exchanges.

Joy leaned back, watching them, somehow, *almost* appreciating these quirks.

"Fullll circus. Chaanceai-illa Thambi[26]," he muttered in Tamil, half-wondering if the gods had a department for irony.

He got that one right.

Though even the gods might struggle to explain how *full* managed to sound so *fullllly* adorable in Indian languages.

Uma caught his words and smiled faintly.

In moments like this, I almost envy humans—their ability to find joy in nonsense, or at least to pretend convincingly.

The day moved on lazily. It always did.

Then came the email. It always does.

It carried an impossible deadline, wrapped in the usual motivational garnish:

---

26 I wish I could translate it someday. Settle for "No chance, bro!" Now, say it like a Carnatic cover of We Will Rock You. Excellent. Whatever you've got? Still not the translation. No chance. Sorry.

Teamwork makes the dream work.

Joy stared at it, trying to imagine whose dream involved weekly ulcers and unpaid overtime.

From the birth of galaxies to this soul-draining fluorescent prison, the stage has shrunk—but the actors soldier on.

Improvising, fumbling, and refusing to exit.

Aadi and Ityadi might have laughed. Or maybe they'd have wept and quit by lunchtime.

This is the beginning of the **Aakār Khand**—the story of your time.

Think this circus can't rival the cosmos?

Stick around.

The 15th Mile

The hut whispered *ancient wisdom* but smelled suspiciously of damp socks.

Its faded walls held too many dreams and too little paint. Above the entrance, a crooked sign wobbled in defiance of gravity, proudly announcing:

Baba Sahajananda
Seer of Paths, Keeper of Simplicity.

Outside, *Shivpalganj*[27] buzzed with its trademark chaos.

Street vendors screamed over each other, hawking vegetables no one believed were fresh.

Cows lounged in the middle of the road with the entitlement of emperors, indifferent to the rickshaw-wallahs yelling as they tried to navigate around them.

Unlike outside, inside the hut, incense smoke curled lazily, filling the air with an illusion of calm.

Baba Sahajananda sat cross-legged on a cushion that had surrendered its shape long ago.

His beard, a waterfall of white, carried the weariness of a man who had seen too many people mistake ambition for destiny.

---

27 Shivpalganj: A nod to the fictional village in *Raag Darbari* by Shrilal Shukla—the greatest satire ever written, even by Shrilal himself. To me, it's sacred text: a book you buy, guard with your life, and never lend because, let's be honest, it's never coming back. My current copy? Third-time purchase. No, I don't want to talk about it.

His eyes, half-closed, hovered somewhere between deep contemplation and a deliberate attempt to avoid the absurdity around him.

Scattered around were relics—or junk, depending on your perspective.

A cracked mirror, reflecting no truths.

Half-melted candles, stubbornly uninspiring.

A precarious stack of yellowing papers, looking more like overdue bills than divine insights.

In front of him, was Vikram Tanwar.

He, too, sat cross-legged just like the Baba, but visibly uncomfortable in his jeans. His posture betrayed a city man at odds with the floor.

Vikram's crisp white shirt clung to his back, damp with humidity and regret.

His face bore the expression of someone pretending to be far more reverent than they actually felt.

The entire room seemed to conspire against him.

Even the bhajan playing on an endless loop felt like a cosmic joke at his expense—complete with an IT acronym open for discovery:

Sahaj Baba's KISS[28] is true,
In simplicity, life feels new.
Banish complexity, let it flee,
With simplicity, set yourself free.

---

28 KISS (Keep It Simple, Stupid): A principle from the development world—the art of making your work simple enough for others to understand, yet stupid enough to keep your job.

Vikram wasn't the type to believe in mysticism. He believed in Excel sheets—which, some might argue, was just another kind of mysticism.

He wasn't here out of faith. He was here out of sheer frustration. Ambition, LinkedIn, and patience had all ghosted him.

Baba Sahajananda was a last resort, a whispered suggestion over chai from a colleague: *"He predicted my transfer before the letter came!"*

The idea planted itself in Vikram's mind and grew like an invasive weed.

"Baba…"

"… ji," Baba's disciple intervened.

Vikram cleared his throat awkwardly.

"Babaji," he started again, aiming for reverence but landing closer to a man arguing with customer service.

"I've worked hard… led teams, delivered results. But the title I deserve… *Engineering Manager*… it's just not happening. What must I do?"

The Baba opened one eye slowly, like someone reluctantly acknowledging the world's latest nonsense. His gaze rested on Vikram, the kind of look you'd give a resume riddled with typos.

"This title you're chasing," Baba said, shifting his weight on the tired cushion, "is it for you… or for those watching?"

Vikram's response was quick, defensive. "Respect, Baba… ji… *Engineering Manager* commands authority. It's not like…" He hesitated, his eyes darting to the floor, as if saying it aloud might tarnish his reputation. "It's not like *Test Manager*." The words tasted bitter, even to him.

The Baba's other eye opened, his expression unreadable. "And what's wrong with *Test Manager*?"

Vikram's jaw tightened, his mind swimming with countless moments he'd been made to feel small—in the company, in society, in life.

He exhaled sharply, frustration bubbling over. "*Everything!* Testing is a disease, Babaji... a virus. It infects every opportunity I've worked for."

The Baba stroked his beard thoughtfully, his face betraying nothing. Then, with a faint smile, he gestured toward Vikram's crisp, tailored shirt.

"*Itne beemaar lag toh nahi rahe ho, beta*[29]*!*"

(You don't look so sick, though, child!)

Vikram clenched his fists, trying not to let the Baba's calm demeanor further aggravate him.

"Babaji, I'm really trapped. Save me."

The Baba's gaze drifted to the cracked mirror beside him. Tracing its edge with his fingers, he seemed to ponder a thought too vast for the room.

"You chase brilliance," he murmured. "But tell me this, beta... are you *truly* that bright, though?"

Vikram opened his mouth, ready to argue, but found no words. His objection dissolved in the silence, leaving only the sting of the question.

The Baba nodded slowly, as if weighing Vikram's unspoken response on a scale only he could see. Finally, he reached into the folds of his robe and drew out a piece of paper, its edges yellowed and frayed with age.

He handed it to Vikram, who accepted it with the reverence of a man convinced he held the solution to all his problems.

The uneven handwriting on the paper read:

---

29 Beta: An affectionate Hindi word for child, not to be confused with its equally affectionate English usage—reserved for half-baked digital offspring that barely works but still need your validation.

At the 15th mile, revelations await.
Follow its path, but don't be late.

Vikram straightened, his chest swelling. "And what will I find there?" he asked, his voice laced with curiosity and doubt.

"*Go*, Vikram Tanwar. The 15th mile awaits," the Baba intoned, his voice carrying a weight Vikram didn't fully grasp.

As Vikram stood and made his way to the door, the Baba's gaze followed him. He had seen many Vikram Tanwars in his time—too many.

"Another one desperate to escape the world of testing," he muttered under his breath, almost pityingly.

With a faint sigh, he added, "I really should raise my rates."

The next day, Vikram stood at the 15th mile.

The road stretched ahead—long, straight, and merciless—disappearing into an emptiness that made him question why he'd bothered coming.

A sign leaned precariously by the roadside, its peeling letters proclaiming:

Mile 15: The Crossing.

Beside it stood a truck.

A rusted relic, existing purely out of defiance.

Its rear was a dusty mural of faded slogans and trucker wisdom. Below the customary *HORN OK PLEASE*, nestled between two peacocks, a message gleamed in bright yellow:

Samay Se Pehle, Bhagya Se Zyada Nahin Milta.

(You neither get anything before time, nor more than what fate allows.)

Vikram squinted at the slogan and muttered, "Even the trucks here have better career advice than my HR department. Is *this* the prophecy?"

Leaning against the truck's hood was the driver.

A man whose weathered face and casual slouch radiated the kind of Zen that comes from decades of not giving a damn.

Next to him, stood a wiry cleaner, humming a tune with infuriating ease—an anthem for wanderers in a place seemingly allergic to answers.

"Wahan kaun hai tera… musafir… jaayega kahan…"[30]

Who's there that's yours?
O Wanderer, where will you go!

---

30 *Wahan kaun hai tera*: If you can, listen to this iconic song from the Bollywood movie **Guide** before going any further. Play it, hum it, or let it roll as background music—you'll find it adds a whole new dimension to the moment.

Vikram's stomach turned. He took an involuntary step back. The words pricked at the edges of his mind, like an old photograph found in a drawer he'd sworn never to open. *Was the song mocking him… or worse, was it trying to understand him?*

The cleaner, noticing the intrusion, paused his humming just long enough to smirk. The pause revealed a chipped tooth that Vikram found… unsettlingly unsanitary.

"Oye!" Vikram called out, his voice carrying the impatience of someone used to barking orders. "This is the 15ᵗʰ mile, right? Baba sent me."

The driver glanced up lazily, squinting at Vikram as if trying to make sense of an oddly placed billboard.

"*Hau, sahib,*" he replied, his tone soaked in indifference.

"Baba sent me," Vikram repeated, with added emphasis, waving the piece of paper like a VIP pass.

The cleaner muttered, just loud enough to be heard, "Another one."

Vikram's patience snapped. "Yes, another one," he retorted, irritation flaring. He turned back to the driver, deeming him the more reliable of the two.

"Baba said *revelations await*. What does that even mean?"

The driver took a measured sip of tea from a glass as battered as the truck itself. Setting it down on the hood with theatrical slowness, he barely lifted his eyes.

"Means what it means," he said, his tone as dusty as the road. "You walk, you see—or you don't."

"That's it? That's the big secret? Just… walk?"

"Some bring big questions, leave with small answers. Others…" The driver shrugged, as if the conclusion wasn't worth finishing and lit a beedi.

"This is ridiculous," Vikram muttered. "I didn't come all this way to be mocked by a truck driver and his… sidekick." He spat the last word like it carried some contagious disease.

The driver's eyes gleamed—not with irritation, but something softer. Pity.

"You city types are funny, *sahib*," he said, exhaling a slow stream of smoke. "Look around. It's all dust... and this dust owes you nothing."

The words stung more than Vikram wanted to admit. "So what now?" he muttered, more to himself than anyone else.

The cleaner, as if bored of Vikram's constant questioning, quipped, "*Ustaad ji, chalein?*" (Shall we go, master?)

"Now we go, *sahib*," the driver said, stubbing out his beedi on the side of the truck, "The mile is yours."

Vikram hesitated.

For a fleeting moment, he thought he saw the Baba's expression flicker across the driver's face—a knowing smile that seemed to whisper, *Go on. See for yourself.*

It was a chilling reminder that wisdom didn't always sit cross-legged in flowing robes.

The cleaner hummed the refrain again, softer this time, his voice dissolving into the dusty breeze: *Jaayega kahan...*

What if the 15th mile wasn't about answers but the questions he'd buried? Was he chasing brilliance, or running away from mediocrity? Vikram wondered as he stared at the prophecy paper, as if staring will turn it into a map.

When he looked up, the driver was gone. So was the cleaner. Even the truck—obviously.

And so, he started walking.

The road, so straight and predictable at first, began to shift.

It didn't change abruptly.

It toyed with Vikram.

The twists were subtle at first, teasing his sense of direction. But soon, they grew sharper, crueler.

Every step felt like movement, but the landscape whispered otherwise. Was he walking forward, looping back, or simply… standing still?

A tree, gnarled and ancient, stood defiantly ahead of him. He was certain he'd passed it five minutes ago.

A rusting lamppost leaned carelessly, its shadow shifting from west to north to impossibly south, as if logic itself had surrendered to the absurdity of this place.

Vikram's eyes darted to the prophecy paper. The ink bled, the words smudging into chaos.

"Baba. Don't play with me," he muttered, his voice barely more than a whisper.

It wasn't a plea.

It was a threat that carried no weight.

The road stretched ahead with the smug indifference all roads seem to have. They don't hurry just because you're desperate.

Then, a figure emerged.

At first, Vikram thought it was a stranger—a shadow against the oppressive light. But as it drew closer, his stomach turned with recognition.

The man wore a perfectly tailored suit, its sharp lines a stark contrast to the dusty, formless landscape.

His badge gleamed unnaturally under the harsh light:

Vikram Tanwar, Engineering Manager.

"Look at me," Future Vikram said, clapping slowly, the sound deliberate, almost theatrical. "The title. The authority. You've made it. Congratulations."

Vikram clenched his fists. "Made it… where?"

"Here. To the place where questions die," Future Vikram smirked. "Do you know how loud silence gets when questions die?" He paused, his gaze lowering for a brief moment, as if recalling an old wound.

The words caught Vikram off guard—he had expected smugness, not this.

"What are you talking about?" he asked.

"Oh, you'll see. When the ambition you chased finally catches you. It doesn't whisper answers, you know… it just laughs."

"Stop talking in riddles!"

"I wish I could say it gets better." Future Vikram's expression softened, a flicker of pity crossing his face. "Was *I* worth it?" he asked, his voice barely above a whisper.

The fluorescent light flared, and when Vikram blinked, the space where Future Vikram had stood was just… empty. As if he'd never been there at all.

For a moment, Vikram considered turning back—but the thought of returning empty-handed was unbearable.

He walked on, each step heavy with doubt. Whatever waited beyond, the road wasn't done with him yet.

The twists in the road became sharper, more erratic.

Out of the suffocating haze, another figure began to take shape.

It was him.

Younger. Brighter. Fresher.

A version of Vikram untouched by cynicism and disappointment, wearing a wrinkled shirt emblazoned with *Debug Life* in faded, ironic lettering.

"You really screwed us over," Younger Vikram said.

Vikram froze in place.

He wanted to turn away, but the road wouldn't let him. His feet felt rooted, as if the dust itself had risen to hold him in place.

"I loved testing," Younger Vikram continued, stepping closer. "You're ashamed of it now. Ashamed of me. What are you even chasing?"

"At least I didn't quit," Vikram muttered defensively, the words spilling out before he could stop them.

"No." Younger Vikram's voice was sharp, each syllable a slap. "You didn't quit—you just stopped trying. What's worse, huh? Giving up or pretending you're still in the fight when you're not?"

"Shut up!" Vikram barked, his voice cracking under the strain.

"Make me," Younger Vikram shot back, bursting into laughter—a sound that drilled into Vikram, tearing at his carefully constructed defenses.

The figure dissolved into the swirling dust, leaving only silence in its wake. As he faded, his voice echoed:

"*You* are the disease that ate us."

Vikram's hand shot out instinctively, a reflex born of desperation, as if he could grasp the fading figure.

"Wait!" he shouted, his voice cracking under the weight of a plea he hadn't expected to make.

But Younger Vikram didn't even pause.

He was gone, but not his words. They clung to Vikram's skin, burrowed into his spine.

A judgment passed—permanent and inescapable.

The silence that followed wasn't empty—it pressed on Vikram's chest, taunting his outstretched hand like a cruel laugh.

The road twisted itself again.

Not to challenge him, no.

It twisted simply because it could.

Vikram kept walking, each step heavier than the last.

Sweat trickled down his back, pooling at his collar and transforming his shirt into a suffocating second skin.

He spat on the road—a gesture more dust than spit—but it gave him a fleeting sense of defiance.

Vikram glanced over his shoulder, half-hoping to spot the truck, the driver, or even the cleaner with his maddening indifference.

But there was nothing.

Only dust, heat, and silence, stretched out forever.

"What do you want from me?" he shouted at the road.

The road, of course, didn't answer.

The dust swirled into shapes that looked suspiciously like faces—his own, his younger self, his future self.

All of them blurred together, laughing at him, their expressions twisted in what seemed like betrayal.

A voice, both his own and not, boomed around him:

Who are you without your ambition?

Who are you when no one's watching?

He clamped his hands over his ears, but the voice seeped in like smoke, insidious and inescapable.

He sank to his knees, clutching the prophecy paper as if it were a lifeline.

Drifting on the wind like a cruel afterthought, came the driver's voice: *The road's got jokes, sahib. It just tells them slow.*

The ink on the paper shifted once more.

The words blurred, then sharpened into something new, as if they'd been waiting patiently for Vikram to finally notice:

The 16th Mile Awaits.

The Naïve

The office wasn't merely a workspace; it was an aquarium. Fluorescent-lit creatures swam in endless, repetitive circles, pausing only to admire their reflections in the glass walls—mistaking containment for importance.

Vikram Tanwar sat in his chair, which groaned louder than his soul.

The clock blinked 9:47 AM, its digits glowing with smug indifference to his suffering.

He drummed his fingers on the desk—not out of impatience but as a countdown to his inevitable exit from this meeting, this day, this life.

Across from him sat Meera Naik, radiating a nervous energy that made even the office plants seem more self-assured.

Her ponytail bobbed like it had a vote in her decision-making process, perfectly synchronized with her internal monologue: *Don't screw up. Don't screw up.*

Meera looked like every fresher he'd ever met—eager, terrified, and utterly convinced this meeting could change her life.

"So," Vikram began, leaning back just enough to make the chair protest louder. "Why testing? And don't recite the manual… I wrote it."

Meera hesitated, her mouth shaping a word but retreating halfway, like a timid swimmer testing cold water.

"I think… testing is essential, sir," she began, her words careful, hesitant but earnest. "It's about… asking… and… finding…"

"And when you graduated? Testing wasn't your first choice, was it?"

"No, sir," she admitted, her voice steady but cautious. "But every job has dignity. That's what my parents say. So… I want to do this well."

Dignity. Vikram hadn't heard that word since the office's last fire drill, when a VP had tried to climb out a second-story window.

Vikram wanted to tell her the truth: *Wait until the system breaks you, kid.*

Instead, he smiled—the kind of smile you offer to someone unknowingly standing at the edge of a very steep cliff.

"Good enough. That's all I ask. Keep it simple, Meera."

It wasn't what he wanted to say.

Wanting things is like bringing a sandwich to a gunfight. Entertaining but pointless.

Vikram had wanted once, too. It had led him nowhere.

"If testing ever feels like a dead end," he added, softening his tone further, "just say the word. There's always… something else."

… far less disappointing, he thought.

This wasn't wisdom—it was survival.

"Thank you, sir," Meera replied, her smile widening just enough.

Was she genuinely grateful?

Or had she just learned how to smile at the right moments? Vikram wasn't sure which was worse. He watched her gather her things, her movements deliberate, almost rehearsed.

Was she truly that naïve?

Meera walked briskly back to her desk, clutching her bag with both hands.

Her workstation was practically a shrine to optimism.

A jade succulent, miraculously untouched by despair.

A notebook too pristine for the brutality of workplace bullshit.

A pen that fancied itself a sword.

On her screen, the onboarding documents blinked back—HR's corporate lullabies, humming words like *Team Empowerment* and *Impactful Journeys*, hoping she'd sleep through the warning signs.

The conversation with Vikram echoed in her mind, but the day wasn't going to wait.

Soon enough, it was time for the morning sync-up.

11:00 AM. The glass-walled conference room buzzed with murmurs from the usual suspects.

Meera sat near the front, her notebook open, her pen poised like a lifeline.

Around her, colleagues settled into their seats with varying degrees of enthusiasm—most ranging from indifferent to mildly pained.

"Three rules for survival," Yogi whispered, leaning slightly toward Meera. "Nod like you're listening. Blink like you care. And forget everything before lunch."

Meera managed a nervous smile, saying nothing as her pen hovered over the pristine page.

At the head of the table, Vikram stood holding a laser pointer. His face carried the weariness of a man who'd already lost several battles with the day.

"Good morning, everyone," Vikram began, his voice trying and failing to sound enthusiastic. "Today, we're discussing how to optimize our testing workflow through collaborative synergies."

Meera scribbled furiously, nodding along like every word carried profound weight.

Yogi watched her with mild amusement. *"Trapped words flutter on paper, longing for their flight,"* he muttered his poetry softly. *"But most of them will go unread, as soon as out of sight."*

Vikram paced, gesturing with the laser pointer as if drawing imaginary maps. "Testing is the backbone of this organization," he declared with the confidence of a man who could spell bullshit without breaking a sweat.

Around the table, heads bobbed dutifully, like dashboard toys jolting along in a moving car.

Meera, eager to contribute, straightened in her seat. For a moment, she felt transported back to a classroom where participation points mattered.

"Yes, sir," she said, her voice trembling with the hesitation of someone trying to fit in—a sparrow in a thunderstorm.

Vikram looked at her, surprise flickering across his face before it was quickly smothered by the mask of managerial indifference.

"Thank you, Meera," he said, his tone hovering between approval and faint pity. "It's nice to see... your enthusiasm."

His smile, however, never reached his eyes.

Meera scribbled furiously, her pen racing to keep up with terms like *synergies* and *optimizations*. She wasn't sure what they meant yet, but they sounded important—like passwords to a world, she hadn't entered.

This was her initiation into the world of testing.

Enlightenment could wait.

Vocabulary came first.

2:00 PM. Meera shadowed Jasleen, the team's SDET.

Jasleen moved with the efficiency of someone who could probably automate her own breathing if she wanted. Her fingers danced across the keyboard, gliding over the keys as Selenium scripts sprang to life on the screen.

Her demeanor was calm, her voice deliberate—a steady metronome against the chaos of the office.

"Code. Automate. Adapt," Jasleen said, her eyes fixed on the screen. "If you can't, you're the weakest link."

The glow of the monitor cast sharp shadows across her face, yet her tone remained detached, almost clinical.

Meera nodded, her notebook already half-filled with meticulous notes. "But *human* testing catches what automation misses, right?"

Jasleen's fingers froze mid-keystroke, the pause sharp and deliberate, as if Meera had just suggested that gravity might be optional.

"Sure," she turned slowly and said finally. "But call it *manual testing*... that's what they understand. Personally? Just call it *testing*. Titles are for business cards, not bugs."

Almost as an afterthought, Jasleen added, "One more thing… Devs? Handle with care. Be nice, but not too nice. They'll think you're weak."

She gestured subtly toward the developers' bay, where Joy was animatedly staring at his monitor, most likely wrestling with some debugging.

As though sensing their gaze, Joy turned.

"Already finding bugs in my code, *Naik*?" he called out, his tone balancing between challenge and flirtation.

Meera's cheeks flushed, but she fired back, "Not yet, sir… but give me time."

A ripple of laughter spread across the room, breaking through the usual hum of keyboards and muted conversations.

Jasleen chuckled softly, a glint of approval in her eyes.

Joy laughed too, though his gaze softened. In Meera, he saw more than courage—he saw innocence.

"Just call me *Joy*."

"I'm Meera. Naik makes me sound like a hero." She delivered the line with a small grin, earning light chuckles from nearby desks.

"You've got guts," Jasleen said warmly, though her tone carried a hint of caution. "Just don't make it a habit. Developers have egos like landmines. One wrong step…" She mimed an explosion with her hands.

Meera laughed, the sound light but genuine. *These are good people*, she thought. *Maybe this job isn't a cliff after all.*

Or maybe it is, Meera. But cliffs have good views, don't they?

Meera walked back to her workstation, leaving Jasleen smiling as she left—a smile that lingered a moment too long.

Jasleen's gaze softened, growing distant for just a heartbeat. *You remind me of someone I used to know*, she murmured to herself, a flicker of memory crossing her face before it hardened again. Her fingers resumed their quiet dance across the keyboard.

Some lessons had to wait.

Too hard-earned to be shared in full.

Too heavy to pass on just yet.

The office thrived on a delicate balance of motion and inertia.

Emails were sent. Reports were written.

Conversations hummed with importance, but deep down, everyone knew, that nothing would change.

Not because change was impossible—but because it was inconvenient.

By evening, the office stood empty.

Desks sat silent. Chairs neatly aligned, like the graves of ideas that never left this office.

The air hummed with the quiet, indifferent rhythm of things that would outlast the people.

Meera sat at her desk, her notebook brimming with notes. She smiled faintly, content with the day's work—small victories etched neatly in tidy lines and bullet points.

As she gathered her things and walked past the break room, a faint conversation drifted out, carried by the stillness.

"Maybe she'll surprise you," a voice murmured.

"Surprises don't last here. You know that," another replied, the words tinged with resignation.

"She's bright. Eager, too," came a softer, more concerned voice.

"That's what worries me. Guide her," came the quiet, measured response.

The Awakening

The interview room was the bastard child of a waiting room and a morgue.

Clinical, cold, and designed specifically to crush souls.

It was as if some sadist with a degree in interior design had asked, *How can we make ambition feel like a hostage situation?*

Jasleen Kaur sat on a chair that felt less like furniture and more like a dare.

Across the table sat three caricatures of corporate mediocrity—accessories with bodies attached.

These were: The Tie, The Rings, and The Hairdo.

The Tie was an unholy shade of orange that screamed *bold choice* but whispered *bad decision*. Its wearer adjusted it incessantly, as if symmetry might somehow compensate for their complete lack of substance.

The Rings jingled with every theatrical hand gesture, their owner moving with the deliberate precision of someone who believed their jewelry deserved its own TopMate profile.

And then there was The Hairdo—a feat of engineering that defied gravity, common sense, and possibly fire safety regulations. Its owner leaned back, spinning a pen as though expecting applause for this vulgarity.

The interrogation began.

Jasleen knew at first glance exactly how this interview would go. *Vikhaani aan thonu naanke*[31], she thought to herself.

"Let's start with something simple," The Tie announced.

Jasleen raised an eyebrow. *Simple? In Delhi? That too in an interview? Let's see how far that goes.*

"How would you implement a Shift Left[32] approach," The Tie continued, "to ensure we catch *every* bug before code hits production?"

---

31 *Vikhaani aan thonu naanke*: Poetry and Punjabi rarely survive translation intact. Sorry. English can settle for: "Fuck you." Literal translation: "Let me show you your mother's father's home." Interpret rest of Jasleen's mumblings with equal care—and caution.

32 Shift Left: A revolutionary, dystopian mind game. You're not just solving problems—you're predicting them like some stressed-out, underpaid Nostradamus. The future's a disaster waiting to happen. Preventing it somehow is your mission—should you choose to accept it.

Jasleen shifted slightly to her left. It felt no different than the right. The chair protested with a low creak, as if asking, *Why?*

"I believe in what I call ESL. *Extreme Shift Left,*" she began, her hands drawing an invisible diagram in the air. "Product concept stage is too late, right? We should start right at the beginning. Let's have testers interview potential CEOs. I think—"

The room went silent for a half-second, before The Rings chimed in.

"Good joke. Let's be serious. At our scale, we need someone who can implement at least 10,000 automated tests using Cucumber[33]. Thoughts?"

Jasleen paused, as if weighing the profundity of the question.

"10,000? With Cucumber? A garden of delights. This horticultural revolution sounds like a great challenge for me and—"

The Hairdo interjected, spinning the pen faster, attempting to generate its own electricity. "We're also moving toward fully replacing manual testing. How would you help us in this transition?"

Jasleen leaned forward, her voice suspiciously calm. "Once I manage to automate empathy and intuition, you'll be all set to fire your *manual* testers."

The Tie froze mid-nod, as though Jasleen had just spoken in a language he'd fake understanding during networking events. The Rings jingled nervously, and The Hairdo finally

---

33 Cucumber: Something you eat—a refreshing green vegetable, often found in salads and spa water. The BDD tool? Something that eats your sanity—a tool that lets you write tests in plain English, so that business people can *totally* read them but *absolutely* won't.

stopped spinning the pen, blinking like a malfunctioning chatbot.

Finally, The Tie cleared his throat. "Alright," he said, forcing a neutral tone. "That's enough for now. We'll be in touch."

The three props resumed their tableau of indifference.

Jasleen stood, the chair letting out a final theatrical screech, and walked toward the exit.

The receptionist greeted her departure with the sterile cheer of a prerecorded voicemail.

"Thank you for coming, Ms. Kaur. Have a wonderful day!"

The words echoed behind her, hollow and unconvincing, as Jasleen stepped into the purgatory of the corridor.

"*Mazaak hi bana ke rakh ditta hai. Gallan automation diyaan te harkataan baandraan waaliyaan.*" she muttered to herself.

(They've turned testing into a joke. All talk of automation. Yet habits of monkeys.)

She wasn't entirely wrong.

The loudest automation advocates were often the same ones quietly clicking buttons like lab monkeys.

Two days later, as expected, the email arrived—with all the charm of a parking ticket.

It grated on her nerves immediately.

"While you have a clear focus on automation," it read, "would you be willing to do *manual testing* for the time being?"

Manual testing.

The words stuck to her like oily residue, leaving behind an irritating aftertaste.

As if intuition, exploration, and creativity could be packed into a single, demeaning label.

It was like calling art "manual coloring."

She muttered the words under her breath, tasting the absurdity. "Manual testing...? *Testing kitthe manual hundi ai? Testing taan testing ai.*" (Testing is just testing)

Womanual testing, she thought wryly. *At least the email could have called it that.*

Her mind wandered further.

"Am I a hypocrite?" she muttered. "Hadn't I been the one telling Meera to embrace the absurdity, to find a way to survive?"

As her voice echoed, her defenses kicked in.

Main? Na, eh saali duniya dogli hai.

(Me? No. This bloody world is two-faced.)

She wasn't the only one mistaking hypocrisy for a maxim rather than a point on a scale.

Still, there was a melody to her Punjabi slang—a rhythm that made even her swearing sound almost sweet.

What if Ityadi spoke Punjabi? Would Aadi have dared to argue, or would he have crumbled under her lyrical truths? Would this world have turned out any differently?

Jasleen shook her head, her reflection in the window mimicking her disappointment.

These scoundrels want obedience, not brilliance, she thought. *They wouldn't recognize real testing if it walked up and slapped them in the face.*

Her eyes returned to the email.

*Fitte hi moonh ehnaa da*a. (Shame on them!).

That evening, Jasleen sat in her small apartment, her laptop glowing with a blank document.

The cursor blinked steadily—patient and unjudging.

It waited.

She thought back to the interviewer's question about *Shift Left*, her jaw tightened.

"Let me talk about this nonsense once and for all," she muttered. The bitterness that had weighed her down began to shift, replaced by something sharper.

Anger, yes—but not at the interview panel.

At herself.

For playing the obedient candidate.

For sitting quietly while they spouted their narrow vision.

For letting their measured smiles define her worth.

Her fingers moved to the keyboard. Words poured out, raw and quick, as if they'd been trapped too long. Each keystroke carried her defiance, her frustration, her truth.

When she finally stopped, her hands ached, her shoulders tense—but her mind felt lighter.

The document glowed on the screen, unapologetic and unfiltered.

It wasn't just a response.

It was a declaration.

The next morning.

Her document was now safely saved—and promptly ignored—in a folder titled *Resumes and Rants*.

Jasleen brewed herself a strong cup of tea and stood by the window. Her mind wandered, grappling with the reality of the road ahead.

Vikram is right, she thought. She took a sip and made her decision. She would leave this strange, ungrateful world of testing behind.

Development. That was the answer. She didn't love the idea, but it seemed simpler than chasing a testing role that valued her worth.

She could write code, sharpen her technical skills, and join the ranks of developers whose jobs came with fewer labels and far more respect.

I chuckled.

I thought Jasleen was smarter than exchanging one trap for another.

The grass is always meaner on this side.

Her gaze drifted to her laptop, where LinkedIn blinked invitingly.

The professional playground, where everyone wore their best masks, pretending to be inspired by generic quotes and recycled wisdom.

But something else caught her attention.

It wasn't a job post.

It was a post by Meera—a short, simple update:

Grateful for my mentor, Jasleen Kaur, who taught me that testing isn't just a job.
It's a skill, a craft, and an art.
Thank you for showing me the way.

The words stopped Jasleen mid-scroll. Her tea cup froze halfway to her lips. She re-read the post, each word feeling both alien and familiar, her chest tightening.

"Meera, *kudiye…*" Jasleen whispered, at a loss for words.

It was a sense of validation.

More than that, it was a sense of concern.

Concern for a young girl with dreamy eyes, tragically looking up to her for guidance.

"I am more lost than you, Meera," she muttered.

A notification popped up, snapping Jasleen out of her thoughts.

It was from Debraj Gohain—or, as the team affectionately called him, The Kaam Debo[34].

She hesitated, her finger hovering over the trackpad, bracing herself for whatever masterpiece Debraj had just unleashed.

69% of Testers just skim the surface. 😉

Sometimes, you've to get in there... deep 🌷*. Really explore those tight spots, and poke around the loose ends.* 💪

Avoid a premature release 🔥*. Slow down, bend the system, and try all angles for the perfect outcome.* 🚀

👉 *Follow me for more juicy insights on testing.*

`#PushHarder #KeepItTight #SweetRelease`

Kaam Debo—the team's unintentional king of double entendres—had outdone himself again.

Jasleen burst out laughing, a loud, unfiltered laugh that filled her otherwise silent apartment. It was the kind of laugh that bubbled up from a place she hadn't realized was clenched so tense.

She scrolled down to the comments, her curiosity piqued. Naturally, the post had racked up over a thousand reactions.

Some were earnest, obliviously praising him.

---

34 The Kaam Debo (Kamdev): The god of love, desire, pleasure and questionable metaphors. A reviewer claimed that Debraj couldn't possibly exist as a character. Then he stumbled upon actual social media content by testing influencers. The Kaam Debo stays—and no, he's not filing any POSH report for this nickname. He loves his team.

Others? Fully committed to the bit, leaning gleefully into the joke.

A few gems stood out:

"Thank you for these penetrating insights."

"You've nailed it!"

"Debo Sutra of testing wisdom. You really have it coming."

Jasleen nearly choked on her laughter.

Debo would probably respond to the innuendos with, *Wow, people really resonate with my deep thoughts.* And he'd mean it.

Debo, with his 75K followers, was a phenomenon in the testing world. He relished the attention, even if his fame often came wrapped in innuendos he never meant to make.

Coming from a lineage of proud chieftains, admiration was in his blood—whether for his testing philosophies or... well, other interpretations.

Jasleen closed her laptop, still grinning.

I am happy for her.

Because sometimes, you *have* to laugh.

Otherwise, you'll cry.

Jasleen didn't need to look for a better circus.

She already had one.

Debo and his accidental innuendos.

Vikram and his prophetic ties.

Joy and his typical developer ego, a thin veneer over a genuine care for testers he could never quite hide.

And, of course, Meera. *Poor Meera.*

The thought lingered in her mind, tinged with affectionate resignation.

Ghatto-ghatt mere vaale baandar change ne.

(At least my monkeys are nice.)

The Kaam Debo

D ebraj Gohain uploaded himself into the elevator, a living, breathing software update in transit.

He stood glued to his phone, his thumb moving with the bored efficiency of someone mindlessly liking posts they didn't care about.

"Hello," he said abruptly.

His voice wasn't warm, nor was it directed at anyone in particular. It felt more like a notification than a greeting.

Meera stiffened, debating whether to respond. She had learned that with Debraj, even pleasantries carried risks.

"Hi," she finally managed.

As the elevator doors opened, Debraj stepped out with the precision of someone whose orbit was dictated entirely by their phone.

No backward glance or acknowledgment.

Meera was left staring at the empty space he left behind. *Even his exits are automated*, she thought.

"Debraj!"

Joy, the Dev Lead, called out from across the room. His tone carried the kind of playful mockery reserved for close colleagues—or favorite targets. "Back from... where was it this time... Timbuktu? How did your sermons go?"

Debraj adjusted the strap of his bag, his faint smile hovering between self-awareness and unshakable confidence. Every applause—intentional or not—was praise in his book.

"Went well," he replied casually, his tone more suited to addressing an audience than a single person.

His phone chimed, pulling his eyes back to the screen. Notifications flooded in like worshippers at his digital shrine.

Nearby, Jasleen leaned back slightly in her chair, her voice cutting through the chatter with precision. "Must be tough… carrying all those likes on your back."

A ripple of muffled laughter swept through the room. Joy grinned, clearly enjoying the exchange.

Debraj glanced up briefly, as though weighing whether Jasleen's comment deserved a response. He decided it didn't.

Meera lingered at the edges of the scene, watching silently. She couldn't tell if they admired Debraj, mocked him, or somehow managed to do both.

Perhaps that was the nature of office banter—a murky blend of camaraderie and critique that no one fully understood.

Her moment of quiet observation ended quickly, though. It was mentoring day, and Uma would already be in the conference room, waiting.

Meera tightened her grip on her notebook, straightened her shoulders, and headed for the door.

The meeting room smelled faintly of stale coffee and dry-erase markers—the twin scents of corporate enlightenment.

Uma stood by the whiteboard, radiating a confident energy that defied the room's muted aura.

"Hi Meera," Uma said with a warm smile. "You're just in time! We're about to dive into Bug Advocacy. But first…" She leaned in slightly, her voice dropping to a conspiratorial whisper.

"Did you hear? Our very own Kaam Debo is back."

Meera nodded hesitantly. "Uh… I met him in the elevator."

Uma laughed, shaking her head.

"No, no, no. You met Debraj. You don't meet Kaam Debo— Kaam Debo meets you."

Her grin turned mischievous.

"But let's throw Yogi into the mix. He needs this."

Before Meera could respond, Uma had already pulled out her phone, typing with the urgency of someone orchestrating a high-stakes heist.

She looked up triumphantly.

"Done. They both will be here any moment."

Meera blinked, unsure whether to feel amused or alarmed.

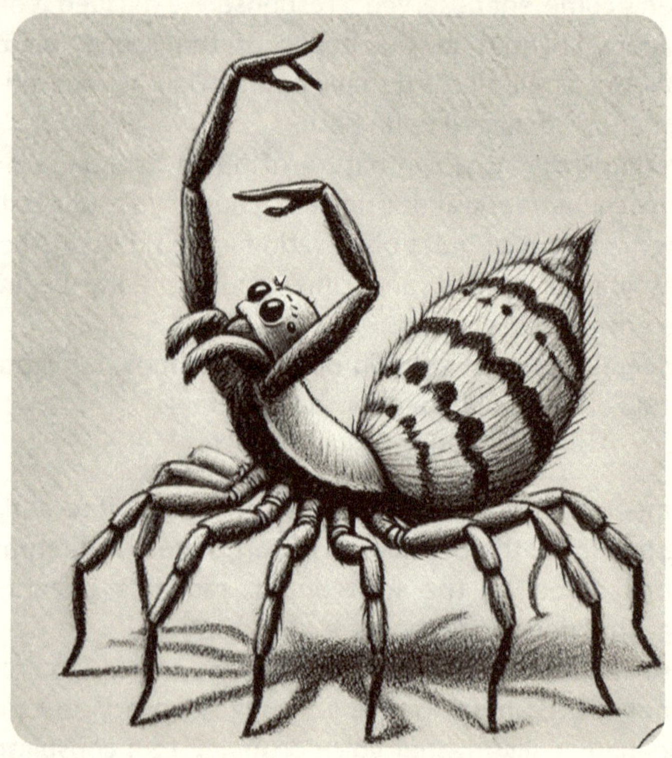

The stage was all set.

True to Uma's word, a few minutes later, Debraj stood at the front of the room—with arms crossed, surveying the space with the air of a commander readying his troops. His phone buzzed in his pocket, a reminder of his digital kingdom waiting to be tended to.

Yogi entered next, his stride unhurried, his expression unreadable. He gave Debraj a mock bow before turning to Uma, his eyes pleading, *Why me?*

"Alright," Debraj began, his tone calm but laden with self-proclaimed authority.

"Today, we'll discuss the art of effective bug advocacy."

He pointed to the whiteboard.

A month-old, unresolved bug report by Yogi, glowed dully in its bland mediocrity:

> Bug Title: Application crashes when user clicks Save.
> Description: App crashes when Save is clicked.
> Steps to reproduce:
> 1. Open app.
> 2. Click Save.
> 3. Observe crash.

Debraj tapped the board with his marker, then turned to the room. "Where's the *seduction*, Yogi?"

The words hung in the air, dripping with unintended innuendo.

Yogi shifted uncomfortably, torn between cringing at being singled out and wincing at Debraj's choice of phrasing.

"Seduction?" he echoed, his voice betraying mild panic.

Debraj frowned, his gaze locked on the whiteboard like a disappointed director surveying a failed audition.

"This isn't a bug report," he said gravely. "It's a death sentence. Boring, lifeless, completely forgettable."

Meera tilted her head. "But it's clear. Isn't *that* what matters?"

Debraj turned to her, his eyes narrowing as if clarity itself had offended him. "Clarity isn't enough," he declared, his tone almost reverent. "A bug report should captivate the developer, compel them to engage. Make no mistake: bug reporting *is* seduction—it's a dance."

Yogi leaned back in his chair, muttering under his breath, "Didn't realize testing came with a pole-dancing module."

Uma choked back a laugh, while Meera's pen froze mid-note, her expression suspended between confusion and amusement.

Debraj, oblivious to the ripple of laughter threatening to break out, pressed on with rehearsed seriousness.

"A *bad* report informs. A *great* report performs."

Debraj erased the original bug title on the whiteboard and, with an air of theatrical importance, wrote:

Save Me: A Scandalous Betrayal

He turned to the room, his expression earnest.

"Have you heard about the peacock spider?" he asked, pausing dramatically. "The male spider dances to impress the female. Just like his dance, a bug report should be subtle, yet irresistible. He shakes his assets. So should you."

Yogi coughed into his hand, avoiding eye contact with Uma and Meera, who somehow appeared far more composed than he was.

Uma quipped, "Assets, huh? Keeping it professional as always, I see."

"Exactly. That's all you've got to grab attention. Assets scream, *Look at me!*" Debraj adjusted his posture, confident he'd just coined the quote of the day, scribbling `#assets` on the whiteboard.

Yogi's cough erupted into a full-blown fit as Uma patted his back, muttering, "Breathe, Yogi. Assets aren't worth dying over."

Uma leaned over, whispering to Meera with a mischievous grin, "Steamy enough for you?"

Meera's eyes widened, her face a mix of amusement and mild horror. Before she could respond, Debraj clapped his hands, startling everyone.

"Next… the description. You're not just describing a problem. You're creating an experience. Developers need to *feel* the bug."

As Debraj launched into his rewritten bug report, the AC unit groaned low and rattling, as if offering its critique.

On the screen, the revised bug description appeared in all its dramatic glory:

> The user clicks Save, hopeful and naive, only to be shattered by a betrayal so profound it could haunt their dreams. In an instant, the application crashes, erasing their work and their faith. It's not just a bug. It's a violation, a moment of heartbreak that demands resolution.

Debraj turned to the room. "See? Now it's not just a crash. It's a story. Developers don't just fix bugs, they fix *temptations*."

Yogi raised his hand. "Debo, it's just a crash. A null pointer exception. Why over-complicate it?"

Debraj shook his head. "And that's where you're wrong. A simple crash is forgettable. But heartbreak? Betrayal? That sticks."

Uma leaned toward Meera, her grin mischievous. "If testing ever goes extinct, Debo's got a future in Bollywood."

Meera bit her lip hard, fighting back laughter until a tear slipped from her eye. Her voice, barely a whisper, quivered with mischief. "Or… in something that's all about assets."

Uma blinked, her grin faltering for a split second as the words registered. "Didn't think you had that in you, Meera. Well played."

"Now… the steps to reproduce." Debraj moved to the final section.

The way he emphasized the word *reproduce* sent a ripple of secondhand embarrassment through the room.

And so, the session went on.

Debraj commanded a room caught between awkward chuckles and outright disbelief.

For all his eccentricity, Meera had to admit that hidden within Debraj's innuendos and dramatics were serious testing lessons.

She glanced at Uma, who watched the scene unfold with a calm amusement, occasionally defusing awkward moments with a well-timed quip.

Meera realized something then: *Uma wasn't just someone to laugh with. She was someone to look up to.*

She stared at the whiteboard, wondering if Debraj had ever learned to read a room. Probably not.

"Men like him rarely paused long enough to check the mirrors. They were too busy admiring their reflections." she muttered to herself.

People like him, Meera. **People**—not just men. You are better than this.

Meera leaned forward, her voice steady but curious. "What if they still ignore my bug report?"

Debraj turned to her, his expression unflinching. "Then you've failed," he said simply, as if the answer were self-evident. "If a bug doesn't get fixed, it's not their fault—it's yours."

As the session wrapped up, Debraj's phone chimed.

He glanced at the screen and read the notification aloud, his voice laced with triumph:

"Bug acknowledged. Fix in progress. ETA: Tomorrow."

Yogi froze mid-step, glaring at Debraj with a mix of envy and existential dread.

"They rejected my report, but they're fixing yours? How—"

Debraj shrugged, the embodiment of casual modesty. "Because I didn't report a bug, Yogi. I choreographed a masterpiece."

The room filled with a stunned silence, broken only by the sound of chairs scraping against the floor as people began to leave.

The absurdity of the session still lingered in the air.

Meera leaned toward Uma and whispered, "Do you think he even realizes…"

Uma smirked, slinging her bag over her shoulder. "Nope. But hey, now you can say you met Debraj."

Back at her desk, Meera glanced at the backlog on her laptop.

As absurd as it sounded, Debraj's bug report had been prioritized. She hated how effective his nonsense was. It made her question everything.

Did substance really matter, or was the testing world just one big, elaborate sales pitch?

Just below it, another bug sat untouched:

'Critical Data Loss During Export.'

The perpetually untouched bug had sat there, quietly mocking her faith in clarity.

Not sexy enough for a left swipe, she thought, the irony sinking in.

The thought twisted uncomfortably in her mind, colliding with Debraj's voice, still echoing like an unwanted mantra:

Developers don't fix bugs, they fix temptations.

The Feathers Too Bright

There's a parrot sitting in a cage, squawking out phrases.

"Who's a pretty boy?"

"Polly wants a cracker!"

Polly's been at it for years, just regurgitating whatever its owner says.

The owner—likely some guy in a Hawaiian shirt, feeding it stale crackers and calling it a conversation.

And this parrot, dear reader?

It's good.

It's nailed the words.

A freaking Shakespeare of mimicry.

But here's the thing—it doesn't know what it's saying.

It's squawking "Good morning!" at midnight, and everyone thinks it's adorable. Meanwhile, the parrot's probably thinking, *What the hell is a morning?*

Then, one day, the cage door swings open.

Freedom. Finally, right?

But does the parrot fly out? No.

It just sits there, staring at the open door, thinking:

Uh, what's out there?

What if there's no one to clap when I say, 'Polly wants a cracker'?

But why are we talking about the parrot? Let's get back to the real story—Meera.

Meera sat stiffly in her assigned seat, clutching a pen like a reluctant soldier handed a sword before an unwinnable battle.

The room reeked of unearned confidence and the quiet desperation of people gambling their careers on laminated paper.

Around her sat a cast of characters straight out of corporate purgatory.

Fresh graduates clinging to the hope that this certification would magically anoint them as *senior* testers.

Seasoned pros scrolling through memes on their phones, occasionally nodding to feign interest.

A man wearing a Bluetooth headset, as if live-streaming critical instructions to a Mars rover.

At the front of the room stood the trainer, a man whose blazer looked like it had given up on containing him years ago.

He adjusted his tie with the precision of someone trying to thread a needle with sausages for fingers.

The slide deck was in no mood to load any time soon. He squinted at the screen—almost patiently.

"Welcome, everyone, to the Global Oversight Authority in Testing... uh, Fundamentals of Universal Certified Knowledge program," the trainer announced, stumbling over the mouthful of words.

Meera squinted, the words on the screen slowly clicking into place. *GOATF...,* her stomach twisted as she pieced together the unfortunate acronym.

Surely, this wasn't intentional. Was it?

The trainer scanned the room, his eyes landing on a senior tester in the second row.

The tester nodded politely—the universal gesture of *I'm too polite to laugh, but I might.*

"This certification framework has, um… apparently been the industry standard for decades." The trainer adjusted his tie again, leaning into his next declaration as if it carried the weight of divine revelation.

"Testing isn't just a job. It's a divine fart—"

He froze mid-sentence, his eyes darting back to the slide. The typo loomed large on the screen, teasing him in **Arial Bold.**

He coughed, his face flushing as he scrambled to recover—while the room, too, reluctantly tried to reel itself back from uncontrolled laughter.

"…*Art*. Divine art," he corrected, his voice a shaky attempt at authority.

Meera hesitated, raising her hand despite the sinking feeling in her stomach warning her she'd regret it.

"If testing is a divine art," she began, cautiously, "how exactly does this certification, um … help us become better testers? I mean, beyond just the theory?"

The trainer paused, visibly taken aback by the unexpected challenge. For a brief moment, it seemed he might actually consider her question.

"That's an excellent question," he replied with a tone that screamed dismissal. "The answer is in section 3.2.4 of the manual. Moving on!"

Meera slumped back in her chair, biting the inside of her cheek to stifle an audible sigh.

What was I expecting? she thought bitterly.

She knew better.

She asked anyway.

Now she suffers.

Meera flipped through the provided manual—a monstrosity so thick it could double as a doorstop.

Unbeknownst to her, the manual's origins were shrouded in a peculiar kind of magic.

Every five years, a secret cabal of testing mystics convened at tropical resorts, to reshuffle this certification syllabus.

The shuffling ritual was less about updating content and more about justifying endless rounds of Mojitos[35].

The trainer adjusted his glasses with dramatic flair, as if preparing to unveil a secret that would redefine the very meaning of life.

"You can shut down your laptops," he announced, pausing for effect. "This is a *brainual* workshop... you know, for thinking."

The term hung in the air like an overripe fruit.

Meera suppressed a groan. *Brainual?* She could already hear Jasleen's inevitable snark: *"Fitte moonh!"* (Shame!)

Coding skills, of course, were treated as entirely unnecessary.

Everyday English words were re-purposed at will, all in the name of creating a "consistent global vocabulary" for testers.

Ancient, irrelevant processes were taught, with ISO, Agile, and context all casually tossed into the same breath.

Questions from the room were either batted away with inscrutable section numbers *"See 2.3.4.5.1"*—or dismissed outright with vague promises to *cover that later.*

"In the last chapter, you said there are two types of testing. Now you're saying there are four." Meera objected, her frustration breaking through.

---

35 A testing certification expert has since contested the accuracy of this statement. According to her, the cabal justifies Negronis, not Mojitos. My apologies for the oversight. If the cabal is reading this, sorry I don't disclose my sources. However, out of love and respect for you, here's a hint: Ginger tonic.

The trainer paused, adjusting his tie with exaggerated calm. "Yes, that was the truth of the last chapter. We're in a new paradigm now. Moving on to section 4.2.1.5.4."

Meera's notes had devolved from genuine enthusiasm into a scattered mess of confused doodles.

Was the system broken, or was she?

She closed her notebook with a thud.

The training wasn't preparing anyone to test software. It was tuning them to navigate the bureaucracy of a profession obsessed with coining terminology and looking busy.

Meera thought back to her conversations with Jasleen and felt a pang of solidarity.

Now, she understood.

Especially the part where Jasleen fantasized about throttling anyone who dared call testing a *'calling'*.

Day 3. As the session finally crawled to a close, the trainer lingered for a moment, leaning against the podium like it was the only thing holding him upright.

His voice dropped slightly, taking on an almost conspiratorial tone.

"I used to be a tester, you know," he said, his eyes glazing over as if recalling a distant, happier life. "Back when we wrote test cases on paper. I thought it would be fulfilling."

He paused, staring at nothing in particular. "Then automation happened. Made me irrelevant. And here I am now..." He gestured to the sad PowerPoint clicker in his hand like it was his jailer. "Writing slides for a living."

He laughed.

A hollow, brittle sound, like a window cracking in the cold. The kind of laugh that says, *This is not where I thought I'd end up*—the laugh of a person whose whole legacy was a folder of slide decks titled:

Final_Final_ReallyThisTime_Final_2_7.

"Anyways, all the best. Don't overthink during your exam tomorrow. Just follow my slides blindly, and you'll be fine."

Just memorize and puke it back. Perfect. Solid advice.

Day 4. The final day arrived, dragging the dreaded exam along with it—the final boss in a game Meera had stopped playing three levels ago.

She glanced at the first question and immediately felt like she was being pranked.

"What is the difference between monkey testing and gorilla testing[36]?" The question seemed to smirk at her, daring her to take it seriously.

The next question was no better.

A *case study* asked her to select the correct response to a bug involving *irreproducible instability during asynchronous calls*. She blinked at the jargon soup.

By the fifth question, she wasn't even pretending to care. Her pen hovered, unsure whether to strike or surrender.

Every question was a new level of absurdity, each one a reminder of how little this process cared about what actually mattered.

The test didn't just despise testers—it was a manifesto for their extinction. It was a eulogy for the testing profession, delivered in the form of multiple-choice obituaries.

Was this test designed for humans or some other species entirely?

Resigned, Meera began circling random answers.

---

36 Monkey testing and Gorilla testing: No, I'm not making these up. Somebody in the testing world did and they did it with a straight face. Reality has a better sense of humor than I do—and a worse sense of dignity.

An hour later, the invigilator handed back the results.

0/50

Meera stared at the score.

Her mind oscillated between screaming into the void and laughing like a villain in a bad soap opera.

"Zero? Not even a pity mark for spelling my name right? What am I—a tester or a bad meme?"

She glanced at the invigilator, half-expecting him to pull out a sign that read, *Just Kidding.*

"Better luck next time," he said, his tone suggesting there wouldn't be a next time.

She sat in stunned silence.

It wasn't just that she had failed—it was that she had failed something so ludicrous it defied logic.

She shook her head, recalling one particularly absurd question: *Which of the following is NOT a testing approach?* The options were shaded boxes in varying colors.

Her stomach growled. "Lunch Box Testing," she muttered, with a smirk. "Option E."

Over lunch, Meera met Yogi at Sandhu's Tadka, the local *dhaaba*[37] that doubled as the team's unofficial therapy center.

Sandhu's Tadka felt alive in a way the training room never could. Plates clattered, and laughter mingled with the rich aroma of butter chicken.

---

37 Dhaaba: India's national institution, where paranthas are thicker than a Marvel multiverse plot. Your arteries won't thank you later, but when that butter-soaked naan melts in your mouth, all you'll think is, "Screw it, who needs to live past 70 anyway?" The flavors slap harder than your grandma's cooking and you earn a bond with your toilet that no one can break.

The naan on Yogi's plate seemed more prepared for life than she was.

"Zero out of fifty?" Yogi leaned back, *chhanna*[38] in hand, his tone equal parts impressed and amused. "That's a statement. You don't fail like the rest of us."

Meera's eyes narrowed. "Is that mango lassi?"

Yogi's expression darkened, as if she'd just insulted his ancestors.

"No. Real lassi. Mango lassi is a crime... just like veg biryani."

"No," Meera shot back, unable to suppress a grin. "Laughing at my score. That's crime."

38 Chhanna: The Punjabi Octoberfest starter pack—a large brass glass brimming with lassi so thick, it doubles as a lung capacity test.

"I wasn't making fun of you. Well, I was… but not entirely," Yogi replied, brushing *paapad* crumbs off his shirt.

His tone shifted, dipping into something more reflective. "The truth is, I bought into this too. Thought these certifications would make me better… or at least valuable. Got three of them and felt like a champ for a while."

He paused, his lassi swirling in the glass like the remnants of his faith in the system only he could see. "Over time, I realized… kissing ass matters more."

Meera was taken aback by the unexpected bluntness. "So, what's the point?"

"The point is… there is no point," Yogi replied, gesturing with gravy-smeared fingers. "They don't need testers. They need parrots."

Before Meera could respond, a voice interrupted from the next table.

"*Keval batiyaane waale tote, bhaiya. Kaatne waale nahi.*"

(Only the parrots that talk, not the ones that bite.)

Yogi burst out laughing, glancing at the waiter who had chimed in.

Balancing a tray of empty plates with one hand, the waiter leaned casually against the table, a grin spreading across his face.

"See? Even *Chotu* knows," Yogi said, gesturing toward him.

Meera couldn't help but smile, though the laughter did little to calm her nerves. "No, seriously. Am I in trouble?"

Yogi leaned back, wiping his hands with a napkin. "Not if Vikram thinks you're indispensable. You're like an iPhone… just without the Apple logo. A harder sell."

Meera frowned. "That's… depressing."

"But that's why you're here." Yogi said, gesturing grandly around the table with an exaggerated flourish. "This is where real testers are made. Yogis."

Meera raised an eyebrow, unimpressed. "Here? At Sandhu's Tadka?"

Yogi leaned back, his grin smug. "Order the butter chicken. Everything in life makes more sense after butter chicken."

She smiled and raised her hand. "*Chotu*! Ek butter chicken. *Ekdum* spicy!"

A young man, just shy of twenty, approached the table, his apron reading "Service with a Smile."

He was tall, perpetually negotiating with the ceiling fan.

Waiters at Indian *dhaabas* are *the Eternal Chotus*[39].

Yet, Meera broke the unspoken rule, defying tradition with a simple question.

"Naam kya hai tumhara?" (What's your name?)

She asked, her voice carrying a flicker of guilt, as though the question had been overdue for far too long.

The young man set down the butter chicken and replied, '*Prabhu, didi.*' (Prabhu, sister.)

Meera blinked. *Prabhu. God.* The name felt... significant. Too formal. Too divine.

She had already *certified* him in her mind. *Chotu.* The label had slipped out instinctively.

Before she could say anything, Sandhu bhaaji's booming voice rang out from the kitchen. "Oye Parbhu, table chaar pe darshan de!" (Hey *God*, Reveal yourself at table 4!)

Prabhu nodded and hurried off, balancing plates with the grace of someone who had long embraced chaos.

Meera watched him go.

---

39   *Chotu* is their proper name. Practically their official designation. They also have a nick name: Chhhsss Chhhsss.

A sound composed of two syllables—a mix of a loud hush and a whistle. It demands practice but becomes second nature over time.

I am the certification that I ridiculed, she muttered.

Yogi was right.

Some things did make more sense after butter chicken.

Back at the office, where reality was reduced to ticked checkboxes and endless emails, a new message waited for Meera.

Vikram stared at the blinking cursor in his draft email.

Three versions had already met their demise, each one oscillating between scolding and encouragement.

"What do I even say to someone who scores zero?" he muttered, his fingers tapping a restless rhythm on the keyboard.

Draft 1:

Meera, your 0/50 score is deeply disappointing. It sets a poor example for the team.

Delete.

Too harsh.

He didn't want her to cry. HR paperwork was a nightmare.

Draft 2:

Hi Meera, let's work together to improve your score in the retake.

Delete.

Too soft.

He wasn't her life coach.

Draft 3:

Meera, I trust you'll take this experience as a learning opportunity.

Delete.

Too vague.

Did this even mean anything?

By Draft 5, he gave up, typing with the resignation of a man who'd made peace with mediocrity.

He glanced around the empty office and lowered his voice as if admitting a guilty secret.

The executives wouldn't know the difference between a good tester and a toaster, but they love their certifications.

The cursor blinked mockingly on the screen, as if taunting his lack of ideas.

He muttered under his breath, "God, I hate this job," before hammering out a final, reluctant attempt:

Subject: Certification Result - Immediate Action Required

Hi Meera,

0/50 is a bold result, unprecedented in the history of Shakuni Software. I am impressed by your out-of-box thinking in redefining failure. At the same time, I recommend a more conventional approach next time - such as passing.

Please retake the exam promptly, as certification is mandatory for client satisfaction and managerial peace of mind. Remember, retake fees are your responsibility.

Don't disappoint me again. Let's recalibrate tomorrow.

Regards,
Vikram

He stared at the blinking cursor.

What would happen if he just deleted the certification requirement altogether?

He let out a bitter chuckle, knowing the answer.

Nothing. And everything.

With a resigned sigh, he clicked **Send**.

His email signature blinked back at him, a cruel reminder of the lie he sold daily:

Failure is just success delayed.

Polly[40] didn't want a cracker. Polly wanted out.

---

40 A reader asked me, Who's Polly? You didn't. Thanks for paying attention. Polly appreciates your vigilance.

The Fallen

Kunal leaned against the counter, equal parts swagger and indifference.

His hair had the distinct look of being styled by hanging his head out of a moving car.

The stubble on his face suggested he'd declared a silent war against razors weeks ago.

His bathroom chappals slapped against the floor with a kind of defiant laziness, the perfect soundtrack to his perpetual state of *fuck-it-all*.

Today, his T-shirt, an off-white relic with peeling letters proclaimed:

Certified Goat[41] Whisperer
Printed beneath it, in mismatched, smaller font:
My bullshitting is corporate-approved.

Meera had avoided Kunal for months.

He was the type to ruin a perfectly good team meeting with just one line and a smirk, then sit back and enjoy the chaos he'd unleashed. To Kunal, meetings weren't obligations—they were social experiments.

However, today, curiosity got the better of her.

Meera's eyes glanced at the peeling words on his T-shirt, trying to decode them. Just a beat too long.

Kunal caught her. "Go on, stare all you want. It's free entertainment."

The T-shirt wasn't just clothing. It was armor, a middle finger in fabric form. Kunal didn't dress for work—he dressed to mock everything work stood for.

Meera blinked. "It's... interesting."

"Too polite to call it crap?" Kunal asked, deadpan. "It's vintage... from my glory days."

Meera hesitated, unsure if he was joking. "I've never... um, we've never really talked," she stammered, cringing inwardly at her own words. "You don't seem like the coffee-chat type."

"Machines are better company. They fucking do what I tell them to do."

---

41 Goat: In case you missed Polly, hope you recall who the goat is. I am counting on you. And just a gentle reminder, up there it's Satyadi as the narrator. Here in the footnotes, it's me, yours truly, Rahul Verma.

"So, this is what you call small talk?"

"Nope. This is my *medium* talk."

A brief, awkward silence lingered. Conversations with Kunal usually ended abruptly. This one seemed no different. But fate wasn't letting them off the hook today.

The air was charged, like two strangers silently debating whether understanding each other was worth the effort.

Kunal gestured toward the coffee machine as it sputtered and groaned, filling his cup with something vaguely coffee-like.

"See?" he asked. "This thing sputters, groans, and still does its job."

Meera frowned, unsure where he was headed with this.

"That's more than I can say for most people," Kunal added. "Excuses, politics, and unfiltered bullshit. You think I hate people because they're stupid? No. I hate them because they pretend they're not."

Meera, now grinning despite herself, said, "Sure, captain. I'll aspire to be a coffee machine."

Kunal shrugged, his tone matter-of-fact. "Why not? Better to output predictable sludge than an unpredictable disaster."

He raised his cup in a mock toast, the coffee machine sputtering behind him in reluctant agreement.

Meera chuckled, despite herself. "That's... bleak."

"Truth is bleak," Kunal said, sipping his coffee, unfazed.

Am I? I often wonder why people assign all negatives to me, when they want to sound philosophical.

Am I bleak, or is Kunal just too lazy to seek my meaning?

By now, I hold a certain disdain for Kunal.

Let's see if he survives this story.

As for Meera, Kunal wasn't patronizing her.

He wasn't sugarcoating his words or treating her like she needed mentoring.

He was blunt, unfiltered, and unapologetically himself—a rare commodity in a workplace filled with facades. It wasn't exactly comforting, but it was real.

Somehow, Meera found it surprisingly soothing.

"So, what made you switch to hacking?" Meera asked.

"It's simple. People treated me like garbage as a tester, so I became something they couldn't ignore… a hacker. Now, I don't give a fuck about anyone. Testers, developers, managers… they can all rot. I'm here to do my job, and I do it damn well. I break stuff… everything they hold sacred."

Meera tilted her head. "But testers don't break anything. It's already broken when we get it."

Kunal paused mid-sip of his lackluster coffee, then let out an unexpected laugh—not his usual pretentious grin, a wholehearted laugh.

The sharp, dry sound startled Meera.

"Sure, keep telling yourself that. Put it next to a motivational poster of a kitten dangling from a branch."

Meera frowned. "But it *is* true! Developers write the code… we just find the problems."

Kunal shook his head, his tone softening slightly. "Look, even my T-shirts are more original than this over-quoted bullshit."

Meera glanced at his T-shirt and couldn't suppress a laugh. "On that… I agree."

Kunal was a bit startled with this rare acknowledgement. He wasn't used to it, and for a brief moment, his façade dropped.

He leaned forward, his voice dropping into something unexpectedly serious.

"They will chew you, Meera. Hell... even charge you rent for being in their mouths. Fight these buggers... at least give them a toothache."

Before she could respond, Kunal added, almost as an afterthought, "And those certifications? Don't waste your time. If you want something meaningful, check out these people."

He rattled off a few names—industry gurus known for their critical thinking and staunch anti-certification views.

Meera nodded, her voice soft, carrying an unexpected warmth. "Thanks."

"Don't thank me yet," Kunal replied, tossing his empty cup into the bin. "They're not saints either."

That evening, Meera dove into the articles written by the gurus Kunal had mentioned.

Their words crackled with energy, tearing apart the dogma of certifications with a boldness that felt almost revolutionary.

They spoke of critical thinking, creative problem-solving, and an open disdain for bureaucracy.

For the first time in weeks, Meera felt a flicker of hope. *This*, she thought, *is what testing should be*.

The articles were sharp and unapologetic, every sentence a battle cry for testers who had been sidelined, dismissed, or underestimated.

Meera devoured them, her fingers itching to jot down notes. *Finally, someone understood*.

But as she read further, cracks began to appear.

The critiques skimmed the surface, never quite plunging into the messy depths of real-world challenges.

Even their boldness felt rehearsed.

It was time for the webinar. The title hovered at the top of her screen:

Beyond Certifications:

Redefining Excellence in Testing.

The guru appeared on screen, a man with graying temples. He had the air of someone who had solved all the mysteries of testing—but wouldn't share them outright.

Behind him, the obligatory bookshelf sagged under the weight of a ton of books. Every title strategically placed to whisper, *Look how smart I am.*

"Testing," he began, his voice deep and deliberate, "is a polymorphic construct, an epistemic activity that interrogates systemic assumptions beyond binary outcomes."

What? Meera blinked, her thoughts racing.

Where are the subtitles?

"While certifications offer a taxonomic framework for rudimentary knowledge acquisition," he continued, pacing theatrically, "true testers must transcend codified schemas and engage in heuristically-driven exploratory paradigms."

A classic move. Make people feel dumb—to make them think you're a genius.

The chat box exploded with enthusiasm:

" 👏 Brilliant!" " 🔥 Mind = blown!"

Meera stared blankly at the screen.

Her pen hovered over her notebook, uncertain whether to jot something down or just doodle a giant question mark.

This wasn't bold.

It was a thesaurus suffering an existential crisis.

She scrolled through the chat, watching the endless parade of emojis and exclamations—wondering if anyone else had noticed that the emperor wasn't wearing any clothes.

So far, it seemed unlikely.

Her skepticism deepened as the guru advanced to his next slide: a Venn diagram labeled *Intersections of Testing Excellence for Self-certification*.

The diagram's three circles—*Knowledge*, *Intuition*, and *Wisdom*—overlapped in a central bubble ominously titled *Transcendence*.

Meera muttered under her breath, "I could use a *transcendent* escape from this testing nirvana."

A brave soul in the audience dared to unmute.

"Sir, how do you manage to stay so humble despite your vast knowledge?"

The guru paused, visibly unprepared for such blatant flattery. "...uh, I wasn't expecting that. I can't possibly acknowledge your comment. Astute observation, though."

Classic professional doublespeak at its finest.

The Q&A session began.

Meera hesitated, her fingers hovering over the keyboard. *Was it even worth bothering?* Finally, she typed:

"What are the practical limitations of your methodology in high-pressure situations?"

The guru paused, reading the question aloud with a faint sneer. "Practical limitations? Limitations are merely contextual opportunities."

He chuckled dryly, the sound like a pat on the head for asking such a silly question.

"This fixation on practicality is precisely what prevents testers from transcending mediocrity. High-pressure situations are merely artifacts of systemic dysfunction, not a flaw in the methodology itself."

Meera blinked. *This... was not an answer. It was intellectual sleight of hand.*

Her question, a genuine attempt to probe deeper, had been swatted away like a fly interrupting a tea ceremony.

The chat, meanwhile, erupted with admiration:

" 🤚 Wow, so deep!" " 🔥 Truth bomb!"

Truth bomb. Is that how humans talk about me now? I half-expected someone to type, *"Sir, you've cured my asthma."*

Meera's skepticism hardened into something sharper.

This wasn't critical thinking.

It was pure theater—a performance designed to dazzle and deflect.

The audience wasn't seeking answers.

They craved affirmation, and the guru was more than happy to supply it.

"A polymorphic realization that I've wasted my epistemic evening," Meera muttered to herself.

Finally, the webinar ended. *Finally.*

Meera looked down at her notes.

Her pages were littered with phrases like *epistemic activity, stochastic universe, and interrogating oracles*—dense, heavy words designed to impress, not inform.

She couldn't help but notice the irony.

The guru had spoken about the importance of questioning at the heart of testing, yet his followers had posed none.

Instead, there was only praise.

Blind, sycophantic praise.

The realization struck her like a slap.

"This is just another cult," she muttered. "a certification-adjacent cult with better slogans."

Certifications and cults weren't so different.

One peddled obedience, the other sold rebellion. Either way, testers were just customers, buying into someone else's definition of competence.

The so-called revered voices in testing weren't the best testers—they were simply the loudest salesmen.

Perhaps she'd been too quick to dismiss certifications. At least their nonsense came with a printed certificate.

Her name lingered in her mind: **Meera**[42].

Her *Ajji*[43] had given it to her, lovingly—a symbol of devotion.

In a world that confused devotion with naivety, her name felt more like a dare than a blessing.

The next day at work, Meera walked up to Kunal.

She didn't bother with pleasantries.

"You're just as bad, you know... as the rest of them."

Kunal raised an eyebrow, caught mid-sip of his coffee. His T-shirt today read:

*Intellectual Masturbation. **Needs No Certification.***

"Good morning to you too," he replied dryly.

"Your whole 'I don't give a fuck' attitude... it's just an act, right?"

Kunal tilted his head, a faint flicker of curiosity crossing his face. "Hey, slow down. I am who I am. What's the matter?"

"I thought you hated being a tester because testers are undervalued," Meera remarked. "But it's more than that, isn't it? You hate the noise. The bullshit. The people who've turned testing into a joke."

---

42 *Meera:* THE devotee. Her faith was proof that long-distance relationships can work—as long as one partner is omnipresent and the other is too into them to notice they're dating the universe.

43 *Ajji:* Grandma: The undisputed queen of perfectly caramelized dosas. She would scold you if you ate a dosa from its edge (rookie mistake). Ajji, with her wisdom, could have warned Meera before Vikram did, sparing us a hefty dose of melodrama in this *khand*.

Kunal was intrigued—or amused, or maybe bemused. One cannot tell when it's about him. "Go on."

Meera hesitated, the words catching in her throat before she forced them out. "You were right... and I hate that you were."

"Right about what?"

"About everything." She waved her hand vaguely, as though the entire world was her point of reference. "The noise, the egos, the cults. It's all just... noise."

Kunal's smirk faded as he held her gaze, his expression unreadable.

"But... you've given up," Meera said, her voice trembling with frustration. "That's the difference between you and me."

"This difference you're talking about, Ms. Buddha... it's just where you stand on the timeline," Kunal said, his tone calm but pointed. "The difference is only in tense. I *have*. You *will*. Give up."

He placed his cup down gently, his fingers lingering on the rim. For a moment, his usual sharpness seemed to fade, replaced by an almost thoughtful stillness.

"Say something," Meera demanded, frustration spilling into her voice.

His lips twitched into something softer, almost sincere.

"You won't like it," he warned.

"Say it!"

Kunal met her gaze, his voice quieter than she expected.

"We're the fallen, Meera. Just bloody monkeys, all of us," he said, his tone heavy with resignation. "I've just stopped pretending I'm not."

The Unsubscribed

No one was dead yet, but everyone was bracing for the bodies to drop.

Rumors had been swirling for weeks. Layoffs were imminent. At first, it was the usual corporate whispers:

"Oh, the client's unhappy."

"The budget's tight."

"Have you seen the CFO lately? He looks like he's aged 20 years."

You know, the kind of gossip that keeps people awake at night—but doesn't stop them from ordering that third cappuccino the next morning.

Uma stood at her desk, arms crossed tightly.

She was the rock, the one everyone leaned on when things went sideways. But today, even Uma looked one email away from snapping.

Debraj, who could usually be found scrolling through his endless stream of likes, sat motionless. No swiping, no smug grins... just stillness.

Jasleen, ever the pragmatist, typed away, her focus unshaken, as if this were just another day in the circus.

Yogi sat silent, his usual quips and bursts of existential poetry conspicuously absent.

Meera stared blankly at the room, clueless about what to expect and what was going on. She hadn't learned yet that in corporate life, ignorance isn't bliss. It's just a countdown.

And then there was Kunal: arms crossed, face blank. It wasn't clear whether he'd chosen his T-shirt intentionally or if the universe just had a dark sense of humor.

The T-shirt announced:
Dogs are Loyal... and Broke.

10:00 AM. The office manager showed on time.

Corporate misery loves punctuality—even in India, where *44 minutes late* counts as *being on time.*

Vikram entered the cubicles area.

Normally, he walked into a room like he owned it.

Not today.

Today, he had all the swagger of a man who'd just realized he'd backed into someone else's car.

He cleared his throat.

That's what people do when they're about to ruin your day.

"Listen up, everyone," Vikram began.

His voice was steady, but you could tell it was taking every ounce of strength not to crumble.

"Management has decided it's time for a..." He paused, searching for the least soul-crushing way to say: *You're fired.* "...strategic alignment."

Strategic alignment: the kind of phrase you slap on a bullet wound and call it first aid.

His eyes darted nervously around the room, as if pleading for someone to nod in agreement—or, better yet, thank him for his creative phrasing.

"I know this isn't easy. Believe me, it's not easy for me either," he added, with the strained sincerity of someone who knew it clarified nothing.

The room fell silent, except for the steady tapping of Kunal's foot.

Everyone else sat frozen, holding their breath, as though staying perfectly still might render them invisible.

But you can't hide from The List, folks.

"Yogi."

The office manager began, clipboard in hand, her face frozen in the HR equivalent of a hostage video. Her voice carried that rehearsed neutrality designed to muffle human pain.

"Thank you for your service. We wish you all the best in your future endeavors."

Yogi rose slowly, his movements deliberate, as though he was carrying something fragile.

His eyes lingered on Uma for a moment before he offered a small, almost imperceptible nod.

Then he smiled.

A soft, knowing smile that carried the weight of everything he wouldn't say.

As he walked to the door, he paused, glancing over his shoulder. He wanted to say, *"It's been a pleasure."* Instead, he quoted Ghalib:

*"nikalnā k̲h̲uld se aadam kā sunte aa.e haiñ lekin
bahut be-ābrū ho kar tire kūche se ham nikle"*

*Of Adam's exile from Eden
Everyone is in the know.
Such greatly humiliated
From your street I had to go.*

Next up? "Kunal." the voice announced.

"Man, you took my T-shirt seriously," he muttered.

Kunal didn't wait for the awkwardness to deepen. His chappals slapped against the floor like a parting shot.

On his way out, he paused at the vending machine.

Moving with deliberate slowness, he punched in the code for a bottle of Thums Up.

The machine groaned in protest but delivered.

Kunal grabbed the bottle, turned to face the silent room, and held it aloft, a gladiator saluting his crowd.

"Cheers," he said, then walked out.

And then... the hammer dropped.

"Uma."

The room froze.

Uma—the rock, the anchor, the one person everyone believed untouchable.

Have you ever seen a room deflate?

That's exactly what happened—like someone had popped the collective balloon of hope.

Meera gasped so hard she practically swallowed her notepad.

Uma stood still for a moment, her gaze sweeping the room, memorizing it. Her voice, steady and unwavering, broke the silence: "Take care of each other."

She turned to Vikram, her expression calm yet resolute, conveying an unspoken message: *I understand*.

As she walked toward the door, the air in the room felt heavier with each step.

Uma brushed against the office plant by the door, accidentally sending it teetering to the floor.

She didn't pause to pick it up.

She didn't even glance back.

The plant lay there, uprooted and abandoned, its soil spilling onto the carpet.

Vikram stared at the fallen plant, something twisting uncomfortably in his chest.

"That's all for today," he snapped, the words more reflex than conscious choice.

That's all for today.

Like it was just another regular meeting wrapping up.

No big deal, everyone.

Just three people losing their livelihoods—carry on!

The office, once alive with the buzz of collaboration and forced cheer, now felt like a tomb.

But life goes on.

That's the sick, twisted joke of it all.

Meera knelt by the fallen plant, gently scooping handfuls of soil back into the pot. The mess on the carpet mirrored the turmoil in her mind.

Uma's steady walk out the door played on a loop in her head, her words echoing louder with each replay: *Take care of each other.*

Yogi's calm recitation of his verse, paired with the defiant slap of Kunal's chappals against the floor, flashed through her thoughts.

They all were gone now, leaving behind only silence and shadows.

She straightened the fallen pot.

"I feel like an orphan," she muttered, brushing dirt from her hands.

The pantry door creaked open, and Joy leaned in, his mug cradled in one hand.

"Cleaning up after management's mess, huh?" he said, his voice quiet but tinged with his signature wryness.

"Uma, Yogi, Kunal... they were the best of us," Meera said, staring at the plant like it was a casualty of war. "And now we're supposed to move on as if nothing happened."

Joy sipped his coffee, his gaze fixed on her.

"Maybe we don't move on like nothing happened. Maybe we move on *because* it happened," he offered.

"You're here, I'm here… Jasleen, Debo, Vikram. You're not alone. You've still got a shot at facing what comes next. You don't move on… you move forward."

She met his eyes, her voice edged with bitterness.

"And what if I can't?"

"Then at least the plant's upright," Joy shrugged. "One thing at a time, right?"

Meanwhile, Debraj was back at his desk.

He spun his pen lazily between his fingers, already crafting the day's tragedy into LinkedIn gold.

The air hung thick with the scent of chai and opportunism.

He began typing.

💔 Layoffs Pin You, But Cowboys Finish on Top. 🤠

Today, they tried to pin me down, like a missionary resigning to relics. But like a true cowboy, I climbed back on top 😉.

Flip the script. 🌷
Grab the reins. 💪
Ride your way back to the top. 🚀

👉 Follow me for more juicy insights like this.

#GrindHarder #StayOnTop #LayoffSurvival

With a flourish, he leaned back, spinning his pen.

"They'll eat this up. What do you think… a thousand likes? Two thousand?" he asked his spider plant.

The plant, however, wasn't buying it.

Neither was the tiny voice in his head that whispered, *They'll eat this up—and they'll laugh at you too.*

Debraj's grin faltered for just a fraction of a second.

"I know. I've always known... how they look at me... laugh at me as if I don't know what they are up to," he murmured. He spun his chair around and grabbed his chai, pretending the voice wasn't there.

His gaze shifted to his reflection in the monitor, overlapping with the draft of his soon-to-be-viral post.

The man staring back wasn't the cowboy in his draft.

Why don't you accept that you are sad? This bullshit post won't fill the vacuum, the voice echoed.

"Okay, fine," Debraj groaned, hitting delete on the draft.

His gaze drifted again to his spider plant. Its leaves had browned at the edges, neglected in his pursuit of the next viral post.

He reached out to pluck a dead leaf, but his hand froze halfway.

Even this plant deserves better than I've given it, he thought.

Late evening had settled over the office.

The office stood empty, except for Vikram.

He sat bathed in the cold glow of his computer screen, staring blankly at the email drafts he couldn't bring himself to send.

Around him, chairs cast long, judgmental shadows on the walls. The machines hummed softly, their indifference more damning than any reprimand.

Vikram had spent years telling his team that testing wasn't a long-term gig. "Move on," he'd said, "Go for development or management. Testing's a dead-end job."

"I told them," he muttered under his breath, as though saying it might absolve the guilt gnawing at his insides.

Vikram's phone sat on the desk, glaring back at him.

He wanted to throw it out the window, but knowing his luck, it would probably bounce back and smack him in the face.

His fingers hovered above the phone, scrolling through his contacts until they stopped on Uma's name.

His thumb hesitated over the call button.

What am I supposed to say?

Sorry I tossed you under the corporate bus, but hey, at least the wheels were freshly greased?

His hand trembled as he set the phone down, in defeat.

What kind of leader am I?

Vikram buried his face in his hands, the weight of the day crushing him. The guilt wasn't just eating him alive—it was chewing him slowly, savoring every bite.

His eyes flicked back to the phone, and this time, he scrolled to Yogi's name.

"Maybe I'll start with him," he muttered. Yogi had always been the calm one, the voice of reason in a sea of chaos. *If anyone could forgive him, it would be Yogi. Right?*

Before he could second-guess himself, he dialed.

The phone rang once, twice, and then Yogi's voice came through, calm as ever.

"Hello?"

"Yogi," Vikram began, his voice strained, "I... just wanted to check in. See how you're doing."

A pause followed—not one of surprise, but of deliberate thought.

"I've been fired before, sir," Yogi said finally, his tone measured. "I'll be fine. Don't worry."

His words were calm, even reassuring, but they hit like a punch.

Don't worry?

Sure. Easy for you to say.

You don't have to sit in this soulless office, staring at the empty chairs of people I've let down.

Vikram cleared his throat, forcing a casualness he didn't feel.

"Listen," he said, fumbling for the right words, "I might have a lead on something... a contact who's hiring. I can send you the details."

Another pause, longer this time.

When Yogi spoke again, his voice softened, but not in a way that eased Vikram's guilt. It carried a weight—a quiet resignation that cut deeper than anger ever could.

"Thanks, Vikram."

And just like that, the call was over.

Vikram set the phone down, staring at it like it might offer an answer he didn't want to face.

There was no fire, no relief in Yogi's response. Just a calm indifference that left Vikram feeling worse than before.

He'd reached out, tried to help, and all it had done was underline how little he could actually do.

Yogi didn't need him.

None of them did.

The truth was, they might be better off without him.

Tomorrow, he thought. *I'll figure it out tomorrow.*

The clock ticked on, indifferent and mocking.

They tell you not to take work home, but no one warns you about taking people's lives with you.

Vikram took a sip from his water bottle. The whiskey burned his throat, dulling the edges of his guilt—but not enough. Not nearly enough.

He reached for the laptop, his fingers hovering over the playlist until they landed on Jagjit Singh.

The ghazal poured into the room, its melancholy curling around him like the smoke of a cigarette long extinguished.

Vikram closed his eyes, letting the words wash over him, drowning the weight of the three empty chairs.

hazāroñ ḳhvāhisheñ aisī ki har ḳhvāhish pe dam nikle
bahut nikle mire armān lekin phir bhī kam nikle

Thousands of desires, each so intense,
That for every one, life would dispense.
Many dreams were realized, yet still,
Too few emerged to fulfill the thrill.

⎯⎯⎯◦◦◦⎯⎯⎯

The Moneypura Chakra

He wasn't heading to the Executive Wing out of ambition. This was damage control. Pure, uncut damage control.

The layoffs—despite his best protests—had gone through anyway.

The announcement had turned LinkedIn into a minefield of performative grief. Self-congratulatory posts were everywhere, stamped with passive-aggressive hashtags like *#GrowthThroughAdversity* and *#TestingMatters*.

Nothing like corporate tragedy to fuel personal branding.

The executives were spooked.

Testing was always the first scapegoat when the numbers turned red, but someone still had to sit there and pretend it mattered.

And for now, that someone was *Vikram*.

This clown, again? Each mechanical sigh from the elevator screamed in protest.

The ancient lift groaned its way to the Executive Wing, as if transporting Vikram Tanwar was beneath its dignity.

If elevators had unions, this one would've filed a grievance. It scanned Vikram with what could only be described as contempt.

Its sensors felt insulted by the presence a man who had willingly chosen testing—of all things—as a career.

Testing!

As a final middle finger, it shut off the AC.

Stew, loser!

Unaware of the elevator's protest, Vikram stared at his warped reflection in the stainless-steel doors.

The face staring back wasn't just tired. It was a cautionary tale—a monument to survival in corporate warfare.

Each wrinkle felt like an unpaid invoice from a life spent pretending that testing wasn't a joke.

Hero, huh? The reflection sneered.

You still clinging to that tie?

Think it's gonna make them respect you?

Why don't you just use it to strangle yourself and save everyone the trouble?

With every floor, Vikram's mask of professionalism stretched thinner, ready to snap.

The reflection wasn't whispering anymore—it mocked, louder and louder. *Please, kill me,* it hissed, venom dripping from every word.

The elevator lurched to a stop.

As the doors clanged shut behind him, the elevator let out one last groan, as if to say:

Don't come back.

The Executive Wing oozed desperation, masked by the perfume of overcompensation.

Marble floors gleamed so aggressively they practically screamed, "We swear we're successful!"

Abstract art littered the walls, each piece more confusing than the last—likely commissioned by an artist who despised them as much as they despised him.

Vikram paused in front of one particularly hideous painting.

It was a blue-and-red monstrosity that probably cost more than his team's annual budget.

"I know it's me who sucks," he muttered under his breath, "but you've really raised the bar, *Moneypura*."

Face reset into his carefully arranged mask, Vikram pushed open the conference room door.

The room dripped with excess.

Gold trim adorned every surface, screaming, "We have money, but no taste."

The sleek obsidian table reflected the executives like a funhouse mirror, warping their smugness into something grotesque.

The execs perched around the table, all taut smiles and empty warmth, like toothpaste models trying too hard.

"Vikram!" chirped the Sales Lead, his saccharine tone teetering on the edge of inducing diabetes. "Perfect timing. We were just discussing the Q4 rollout."

Vikram forced a smile so polished it could've been part of the décor.

"Always a pleasure," he lied, the words sliding out like well-oiled nonsense.

"Let's talk priorities," the Sales Lead continued, all teeth and zero sincerity. "With the recent… strategic reallocations in testing, how do we maintain quality without, you know… actually investing in it?"

Vikram wanted to laugh, but he'd learned long ago that laughing in these meetings was just another way to dig your own grave.

Instead, he tilted his head like he was deep in thought.

"Quality is always a priority," he deadpanned.

"We need cost-effective quality," chimed in the Marketing Head, her smile stretched so tight it looked like it physically hurt. "Surely there's a way to deliver quality without the inconvenience of perfection."

Ah, yes. Perfection. The inconvenience of not sucking. Vikram gave a slight nod, his expression one of mock contemplation.

"Absolutely. The key is to focus on perceived quality. Customers don't want perfection—they want the illusion of it. Bugs, when framed correctly, can even be delightful. Think of them as… interactive features."

The room buzzed with forced agreement.

The execs nodded like bobbleheads, their smiles plastered on as though they'd just witnessed brilliance.

The CEO spoke, his tone smooth but burdened by carefully chosen words.

"Vikram," he began, steepling his fingers. "Your insights, as always, are invaluable. And we've been exploring how to best leverage your… considerable talents. Your transformative leadership has prompted us to rethink the role entirely. In light of your contributions, we believe it's time to broaden your horizons. What are your thoughts on transitioning into an Engineering position?"

There it was.

The carrot dangling just close enough to tempt, but far enough away that you'd have to sell your soul to reach it.

Vikram had wanted this for years.

A real engineering role meant control—or at least it promised respite from the perpetual scapegoating of testing.

But he wasn't stupid.

He knew exactly what this really meant: *We're phasing out your job, but hey, let's pretend it's a promotion!*

His smile widened as his eyes narrowed, a silent warning shot across the room.

"I appreciate the opportunity," he said, each word calibrated like a chess move.

I see your hand on the knife, but I'm not letting you twist it... just yet. "Building teams is my passion, but even magicians require the props. Without testing, even the illusion of quality becomes impossible to sustain."

The CEO's smile didn't falter, but Vikram caught a flicker of tension in his eyes.

The execs nodded eagerly, keen to move on, and the meeting wrapped with the usual wave of empty promises and fake enthusiasm.

Vikram had spoon-fed them a carefully rationed dose of corporate compliance.

That was the trick:

Play dumb just enough to keep the paycheck coming, but not so dumb that they stop being scared of losing you.

He had no intention of being their sacrificial lamb.

As the meeting wrapped up, the Sales Lead leaned in one last time, his grin just a shade too smug.

"Between us, testing doesn't matter. We just need the investors clapping. That's all. Keep the illusion alive until Q4, yeah?"

Finally, some honesty.

Too bad it felt like arsenic served in a champagne flute.

Vikram's smile stayed plastered in place, but inside, something twisted painfully.

Keep the illusion alive until Q4?

Fine.

Just don't blink, or you'll miss the real show.

The elevator seemed even more offended now, as if the stench of the execs had clung to him. Its groans grew louder as it spat him back to where he belonged.

Back on the floor, the whispers began.

"What's the damage this time?" someone whispered, their eyes darting toward him.

"He's back too fast. Can't be good," another quipped, ducking behind their monitor like his presence was contagious.

Let them talk, Vikram told himself. *Survivors don't explain. Fixers don't apologize.*

His pace slowed as he passed Uma's desk, memories tugging at his feet.

Her chair sat slightly askew, as though she might return at any moment. The chipped '#1 Tester' mug sat untouched, a faint ring of dried coffee clinging to its base.

His fists tightened in his pockets as he released a slow, deliberate breath.

Almost there, Uma. Almost.

The Party

The office, once a monument to monotony, had transformed into something almost magical.

Twinkling fairy lights had staged a quiet coup against the tyranny of fluorescents. Five-star pastries lounged smugly on silver platters, mocking the vending machine's stale, forlorn sandwiches.

At the heart of it all stood Vikram, the newly minted *Engineering Manager* who had, somehow, turned layoffs into a celebration.

The man had spent weeks wrestling with guilt and corporate red tape to bring Uma and Yogi back. Now, Uma was the new Test Manager.

Kunal had slipped through his fingers, despite Vikram's best attempts to bring him back too.

It wasn't everything, but it was something.

Vikram stood among the pastries and platters like a reluctant prophet—celebrating for doing what shouldn't have needed doing in the first place.

Leaning against a pillar, drink in hand, he scanned the room with quiet satisfaction.

He caught a glimpse of Yogi laughing. It was real laughter, not the sardonic chuckle he'd mastered.

Uma was mid-conversation, her voice radiating the unmistakable confidence that defined her.

"If corporate life gave lemons," Vikram muttered to himself, "I turned them into a damn cocktail."

By the food table, Yogi stood, drink in hand.

Gazing into the void of his thoughts—or maybe just the kebabs. Same vibe.

He looked… content. Not angry, not resigned… just quietly at ease.

Yogi raised his glass in a quiet toast.

Not to the company, but to Vikram.

This was better: working for people, not institutions.

Meera clung to her soda like a flotation device in a sea of corporate absurdity.

Office politics, layoffs, and now this fever dream of a party—it was all too much.

It felt like the universe had lost the plot.

Her wide eyes flitted from person to person, silently trying to decode what fresh madness she'd signed up for.

Is this what they meant by team culture?

Debo lingered near the kebabs.

Phone in hand, he live-posted the absurdity of corporate celebrations:

My manager's got my back. 🛡 And I love it. 🚀
#CorporateZen #KebabGoals #LayoffLuxury

Notifications poured in as fast as the skewers vanished, and Debo grinned.

The algorithm loved cynicism more, but absurdity did well too.

Something was undeniably off about Joy tonight.

Usually, Joy was background noise—sarcasm and passive-aggressive quips blending into the office hum.

But tonight?

Joy looked... animated. The kind of animated that only comes with too much booze. And that was never a good sign.

What followed would go down in history as *The Incident*— the moment that got drinking permanently banned at office parties.

Joy slammed his drink on the table with the flair of a *Kollywood*[44] hero gearing up for a dramatic monologue.

---

44 Kollywood: The informal name for Tamil-language film industry in India. A reviewer suggested removing this chapter, but it remains— for my love of Rajni sir and because my son's name is Joy. Joy stays.

The room froze.

Heads turned.

Drinks hovered mid-air.

"Alright!" Joy barked, raising a finger with the confidence of someone who had just discovered free therapy. "We need to talk... about this whole *testing* thing!"

He paused—either for dramatic effect or because the room was spinning, and he needed a moment to steady himself.

"I can't hold it in anymore. I've had enough of this bullshit. *All of it.*"

He gestured wildly, words tumbling out faster than his drink-soaked brain could process.

"You don't get it," Joy said, wagging his finger. "We create. We developers bleed our souls into code. It's like... it's like our child."

He suddenly cradled an imaginary baby in his arms, swaying slightly. "*Aiyo enn chellaaa kutti kutti kutti*[45]," he cooed, his voice soft and absurdly tender. The shift was so jarring, half the room choked on their drinks.

Joy's tone snapped back, sharp and accusatory.

"And then you lot..." He waved vaguely at everyone. "You poke at it, tear it apart, call it ugly. Do you even know how that feels?"

The room fell dead silent, except for Debo, who whispered to Meera, "I can't decide if this is tragic or groundbreaking content."

---

45 *Aiyo enn chellaaa kutti*: An affectionate phrase for a little one in Tamil. It probably also means the same in my language as well as yours too. It's a part of the secret, universal "mother tongue" used to soothe infants. The babies, wide-eyed, seem to say, *What? Do it again.*

Uma pinched the bridge of her nose, muttering, "Not again."

But Joy wasn't done. He pointed dramatically at Vikram, his voice cracking.

"And you! You lead them! Do you even like children? Do you?"

No one could tell if Joy was accusing Vikram of being a bad manager, a bad parent, or both.

The room held its breath.

For a moment, Joy wasn't the snarky developer they all knew. He looked like a man grappling with a world that had spun off its axis.

"I hate you… a lot… I mean…" He paused, his voice softening, words barely holding together. "…sometimes. But I hate *them* more. Those assholes upstairs…"

He jabbed a finger toward the ceiling, as though corporate power lived directly above. "…who fired my friends like they were nothing."

His gaze shifted to Uma and Yogi. His voice dropped to a hushed tone.

"They treated you like numbers. But you… you're my family. Kunal too," he said, Kunal's name almost stuck in his throat.

The room was utterly still now, everyone hanging on his words. Even the kebabs seemed to shiver in agreement.

"You're a mess, bro," Debraj said with a shrug.

Joy swayed, his frown deepening as he fumbled.

"You know, we… the testers…" He stopped, frowning harder as though the words didn't sit right.

"Wait, wait… I mean *you*, you guys… no, *we*…" He gestured vaguely, as though swatting pronouns into place.

Then he laughed—a sudden, self-deprecating chuckle that cracked the tension in the room.

"Damn, I'm drunk."

Laughter rippled through the room, hesitant at first, then growing.

Uma smiled faintly, shaking her head like a parent watching their kid make a fool of themselves at a school play.

Just when everyone thought it was over, Joy waved his hand dramatically, nearly toppling his glass.

"You lot… you testers…" He squinted, as if the word itself was an ancient curse he was struggling to pronounce.

"You've got it rough, don't you?"

He paused, waiting for applause or agreement, but the room stayed silent. No one dared interrupt his drunken revelation.

"As Gandhi said, testers are like… janitors."

Uma folded her arms, a mix of amusement and mild offense flickering across her face.

"Joy, I swear, if you compare us to janitors…"

"No, no!" Joy interrupted, his glass waving wildly.

"You're not like janitors… janitors clean up messes. You're janitors with a vendetta. You don't sweep it away… you shove it in our faces and watch us trip over it. That's badass!"

He stopped, squinting again as though hunting for the right metaphor—the perfect insult wrapped in a compliment.

"You're… janitors with the superpower of justification. You justify your job every damn day. Day after day… after day… after every single fucking day!"

Uma muttered under her breath, "I'm going to murder him."

Joy stumbled forward.

"You're heroes!" he declared loudly, his voice cracking with conviction. "But like… reluctant heroes. Batman without the budget. *Garibon ke Batman*[46]."

It was clear Joy was trying to say something meaningful. Something profound. But he had picked the wrong day—and the wrong blood-alcohol level—to do it.

"Developers," Joy continued, his words slurring but his conviction somehow intact, "…we just code and the world says…, 'Good job, here's your paycheck.' No questions asked. No explanations."

He swayed slightly, his glass wobbling dangerously. "And here you all are… fighting for your right to exist… and…"

A few exchanged surprised glances.

Was Joy actually complimenting them, or was this just drunken rambling laced with accidental sincerity?

"You guys don't even get the damn respect you deserve. And that's just so fucked up. Without you…" Joy paused, squinting at nothing in particular as if trying to recall where he was or why he started this rant in the first place.

"*Without* you… I'm a mess. My code's crap. *With* you, it's…" He stopped again, his face lighting up. "…still crap!"

The room froze. Glances darted between Joy and each other, waiting for someone to break the unbearable silence.

And then, like a dam bursting, the room erupted into laughter—a chaotic mix of relief, disbelief, and pure absurdity.

Even Uma, who had been on the verge of throttling Joy, cracked a smile.

---

46   *Garibon ke Batman:* A phrase that translates to Batman for the poor. Unlike the English phrase, which sounds like a well-meaning NGO, the Hindi version implies a hilariously shoddy Batman knockoff, complete with a cape that probably doubles as a bedsheet.

Joy grinned, utterly oblivious to the chaos he'd caused. "... But it's the kind of crap we can live with. And that's something. That's... everything."

Joy's drunken outburst was raw, unscripted and shockingly out of character for the developer who usually kept testers at arm's length.

"I love you, man," Joy proclaimed.

Before anyone could react, he staggered forward and planted a loud, sloppy kiss on Yogi's cheek.

Yogi, ever the calm philosopher, patted Joy's shoulder. "Alright, alright. Let's not get sentimental. It's weird."

Joy spun around, jabbing a finger at Debraj, nearly tripping over his own feet in the process.

"And Debo!" he bellowed, his voice a slurred mix of drunken affection and accusation. "You're a pain in the ass. But you're *my* pain in the ass."

The room erupted in laughter, the evening's tension dissolving into genuine amusement.

Joy's glass was nearly empty, but his resolve brimmed at full capacity.

He swayed dangerously close to the buffet table, steadying himself with one hand on a tray of untouched kalmi kebabs.

His eyes locked onto Vikram like a hawk spotting a particularly guilty rabbit.

"Mr... *Engineering*... Manager...!" he called, dragging out each word with exaggerated flair.

Vikram froze mid-sip. "Here we go," he muttered.

"You're like one of those tragic movie guys," Joy slurred, his gestures growing increasingly erratic. "Act One... Big screw-up. Layoffs. Guilt. Betrayal... all of it... But then! Act Two. You try to fix it... you bring people back... you throw a party. You pretend to care."

The room went uncomfortably silent. Vikram raised an eyebrow, his grip on his drink tightening.

"But you do care, don't you?" Joy's voice softened unexpectedly, catching everyone off guard. "That's the twist. You care so much... it's almost annoying."

He paused, almost thoughtfully.

"You're... you're just another cog in the big, dumb machine, Vikram..." Joy continued, his tone both resigned and oddly affectionate.

Vikram blinked, his mask of calm slipping for a fraction of a second.

"But," Joy raised a finger triumphantly, swaying slightly, "you're the only cog trying to turn the other way. For that I love you..."

Vikram's carefully maintained composure cracked, emotion flickering across his face.

"Sorry, Yogi... but I need to kiss Vikram too." Joy stumbled toward Vikram.

Uma, arms folded and eyebrow raised, muttered just loud enough for everyone to hear, "Let's get Joy out of here before HR decides... they want to kiss him too."

Joy staggered forward again, arms spread wide like a prophet unveiling the ultimate truth.

"We're all in this together!" he declared, his words slurring slightly but carrying surprising conviction. "Don't let anyone forget that."

The room fell silent.

Joy's drunken ramble had unexpectedly become the emotional crescendo no one expected.

"*Challo, Joy bhaaji. Uber aa gayi,*" Jasleen muttered, already pulling out her phone. (Let's go, Joy bro, Uber cab has arrived.)

Joy staggered toward the door, pausing dramatically to turn back, grinning like a man convinced he'd just solved world peace.

"Love you guys… seriously. Even you… Uma… but you scare me."

Uma smirked. "Flattering, Joy. Truly inspiring."

The room exhaled.

The party slipped back into its chaotic rhythm, the moment fading into a blur of clinking glasses and half-drunk laughter.

Meera stood by the drinks table, still trying to process what she'd just witnessed.

Joy's drunken sermon was a paradox—a critique of their work, wrapped in an undeniable defense of their worth.

Strangely enough, these were the most honest, comforting words she'd heard since joining the company.

Her gaze lingered on the team.

Flawed, chaotic, and buzzed just enough to forget their troubles, but undeniably a team.

Maybe—just maybe—this beautiful chaos was worth sticking around for.

Across the room, Vikram's gaze caught Uma's.

Without a word, he raised his glass in a silent toast.

She nodded back, her smirk softening into a genuine smile.

Jasleen let out a resigned sigh.

She shook her head fondly, steering Joy away from a night of questionable choices.

Love you, bhaaji.

The Mirage

The announcement landed like authentic Italian pizza at a desi fast-food joint—lost in translation, underappreciated and violently unwelcome.

We're sending you all to a testing conference!

The room reacted with the enthusiasm of a mandatory fire drill.

Meera, however, sat upright, her eyes wide with a glimmer of hope bright enough to light a cubicle.

"This is it," she thought, her pulse quickening. "A real chance to see what testing looks like in the big leagues.

They wouldn't send us to this thing if it wasn't important...
right?"

Meera's optimism was almost endearing. Despite all
the evidence, she, true to her name, remained devoted to
testing.

Joy, slouched so low in his chair he could've been mistaken
for abandoned office furniture, snorted.

"Sure. At least it's better than the two-hour webinar on
mindfulness in the workplace. I'm still recovering."

Meera held her ground, her optimism burning bright, even
as the room radiated apathy.

"It can't all be bad," she said, her voice cracking just
slightly.

Yogi nodded thoughtfully. "The food's great at this
conference."

"Yeah," Joy shot back, his sarcasm sharp enough to cut
glass, "and I bet the keynote speaker is some self-proclaimed
'Testing Guru' who can't find his own PowerPoint file without
a search bar."

Meanwhile, Debraj was in his own world, hunched over
his phone, typing furiously:

Packing my bag for the world's most stimulating testing
conference.
It's going to be intense, sweaty, and full of surprises. 🧳 🔥
#ConferenceReady #TestingPleasure

Debraj leaned back, satisfied, and declared, "It's gold."

Joy, mid-sip of coffee, nearly choked. "Intense? Sweaty?
Really, Debo?"

Debraj waved him off, his tone unbothered.

"Relax. It's the internet. Half of it is bots, the other half is
you. You love this stuff, right?"

The conference venue was as extravagant as a wedding for a second cousin you don't like—large, gaudily decorated, and cold enough to store vaccines.

Polyester lanyards hung limply around necks, their bright colors doing little to disguise their cheap construction. Most wouldn't survive till lunch.

The carpet, an aggressive shade of corporate gray, was patterned with swirls. An abstract nod to innovation, or maybe just a clever way to conceal coffee stains.

The sound system crackled intermittently, groaning under the weight of a thousand bad PowerPoint slides.

It seemed almost sentient in its protest, as if asking, *Why am I here?*

A painfully cheerful announcement boomed, startling everyone: "The keynote will begin in five minutes. Please proceed to the main hall!"

Meanwhile, attendees shuffled sluggishly, weighed down by swag bags filled with stress balls and cheap pens.

The main hall was colder than a server room[47].

Rows of uncomfortable chairs stood in military precision, their rigid backs daring anyone to find comfort.

Onstage, a single spotlight illuminated a podium, flanked by two massive screens looping stock footage of endlessly turning gears.

For a conference marketed as *next-gen*, the setup reeked of an outdated testing infomercial.

---

47 Server rooms are the corporate equivalent of a mini-Antarctica, where the machines are pampered like royalty, while the IT penguins shiver like peasants. They are colder than your manager's response to budget requests.

Posters of speakers lined the walls, their faces frozen in overly enthusiastic grins. They flaunted titles with generous garnishing of words like *guru, ninja, monk.*

"Clowns," Joy muttered as he walked in. "Let the costume party begin."

Meera adjusted her lanyard, scanning the crowd with a blend of curiosity and cautious optimism.

Testers from all over the world mingled in subdued tones, nodding solemnly at banners bearing words like *Innovation, Agility,* and *Automation.*

See? Meera thought, clutching her notebook like a talisman against cynicism. *These are serious people here to learn. It can't all be bad.*

"Is it true if we say *Agility* three times, an Agile Coach appears," Joy asked, eyes wide with mock sincerity.

"Here? You just mumble it once, and three of them are breathing down your neck." Yogi shot back, sending Joy into a coughing fit.

The keynote speaker stood at the podium, his face glowing with a misplaced zeal—like he thought he was delivering the Gettysburg Address of testing.

His mic, however, was in no mood of hearing *"quality"* again. Clearly allergic to the word, it let out a piercing squeal every time he uttered *quality*.

"Testing," he began, his voice booming over the mic's irritated protests, "isn't just about finding bugs. It's about ensuring—"

Squeeeeeeak[48]*!*

The audience flinched, their expressions ranging from mild discomfort to outright despair.

Joy leaned over to Yogi. "See? Testing does not ensure a damn thing. Even the mic knows this."

Oblivious to the auditory assault, the speaker soldiered on. *Squeeeeeak!* "—is everybody's responsibility and—"

Meera glanced around the room, hoping to spot someone equally horrified.

The audience was divided.

Half nodded along as though attending a TED Talk, their faces glowing with a reverence usually reserved for self-help gurus. The other half typed furiously on their phones, their screens hiding God-knows-what.

---

48 Squeeeeeak: A tester told me this was a spelling mistake. He reported the bug to the mic, demanding it learn proper English. The mic, laughed—then *squeeeeeeaked* even louder, adding more 'e's for good measure. When will developers start taking testers seriously? Bad mic.

The speaker, apparently sensing (or imagining) the energy in the room, raised both arms dramatically.

"Now, let's say it together, everyone! What are the three sacred pillars of testing?"

Squeeeeeak! Squeeeeeak! Squeeeeeak!

Joy buried his face in his hands, muffling a laugh. "Quality's bleeding out."

The next session promised something "innovative":

What Pottery Taught Me About Testing.

"This has got to be satire," Joy said, flipping through the agenda. "The testing world really can't resist stretching metaphors until they snap, can they? I'm half expecting 'Quality Assurance and the Art of Origami.'"

"We had *Orgasm* at last year's conference." Yogi chuckled.

Joy choked on his coffee, wheezing with laughter until he realized Yogi wasn't kidding. His eyes widened. "You're serious?"

Yogi nodded solemnly. "From quality to climax... they covered it all. It was... illuminating."

The speaker, a man in his late 40s who had clearly never touched a lump of clay in his life, launched into a rambling monologue.

Meera faltered. "He's just... comparing random things to testing. What does this even mean?"

"Testing, much like pottery, is an art form. It demands patience, care, and the ability to mold quality from raw material." the speaker continued.

Debo was on fire now:

Pottery = Testing. Smooth hands, right pressure, careful fingers.
 #MetaphorPotty

Debo leaned back, smugly admiring his work.

Within minutes, Debo's typo was hailed as deliberate genius, with followers flooding his post with comments like, "Brilliant wordplay!" and "Insightful as always, Debo!"

Even Joy winced. "Debo, you're going to get us banned from conferences."

The subsequent session was no better.

A speaker kicked things off with: "Testing is like jazz: it's all about improvisation."

Meera shot Joy a look, and he mouthed, "Kill me now."

By the time they hit the breakout session, *Testing is Like Gardening - Nurturing Quality from the Soil Up*, even Meera was running low on hope.

She now began to wonder if her devotion to testing was just another elaborate joke. "Why are we even here?" she whispered, half to herself.

Pottery. Jazz. Gardening.

Testing seemed to be everything—*except testing itself*.

Her frustration deepened as the crowd nodded along and clapped.

Am I the crazy one here? she wondered.

She had been expecting rigorous discussions, real insights—anything but this shallow parade of buzzwords and half-baked analogies.

Yogi leaned over. "Still holding out for the breakout sessions?"

"No," Meera replied flatly. "Maybe just the panel discussion post-lunch."

The audience shuffled out, dazed and hungry, like survivors of a particularly bad team-building exercise.

Lunch was supposed to be a break, but the buffet line resembled a gladiatorial arena.

Testers jostled for position, elbows flying, plates wobbling under towers of biryani.

Poor *samosas* were slapped aside by *naans*, while tamarind *chutney* waged war on unsuspecting *rasmalai* in more than a few plates.

Someone yelled, "Save me a *gulab jamun!*" like it was their dying wish.

Meera, observing the carnage from a safe distance, shook her head. "This buffet line is the most competitive thing I've seen all day."

Sponsor booths circled like vultures, watching testers battle for carbs.

Engineers who usually haggled over salaries were now cheerfully trading their 15 minutes for a 2-rupee pen.

Meanwhile, Debo posted another gem:

```
Testing conference lunch: Grab it while it's fresh and hot.
Nobody likes a limp hotdog.
#TestingMeatsReality #LettuceEatTogether
```

Joy wandered back to the table with three plates stacked like a Jenga tower.

"You guys tried the dessert?"

"You know, this is the one thing they've nailed. The food." Yogi mused, taking another bite of his perfectly spiced *biryani*. "Probably because it's the only thing they actually did not directly control."

As they sat in the chaos of half-eaten plates and the hum of awkward small talk, Meera stared silently at the dessert tray.

Somewhere, a distant voice crackled over the sound system: "Join us after lunch for a revolutionary panel on *AI in Testing: The Future of Excellence*."

Meera pushed her plate aside and stood abruptly.

"Where are you going?" Joy asked, startled.

"To find out if there's any truth in this mirage," she replied, her voice steady, though her eyes betrayed the storm brewing within.

The Crack

"AI in Testing: The Future of Excellence,"** proclaimed the panel title in bold, confident letters.

Artificial Intelligence had become the darling of the testing world, especially with the advent of GenAI[49], which promised to make advanced technology accessible to everyone.

---

49 GenAI: Generative Artificial Intelligence. It can write a book in minutes. Will it make sense? Who cares. For perspective: I wrote this book in two months, and it definitely makes more sense. Right? ...Right?

Understanding AI was entirely optional—a perfect match for conferences, which thrived on jargon, spectacle, and the seductive allure of exaggerated potential.

The panel was announced with a flourish. The moderator strode onto the stage with the swagger of someone introducing a Nobel committee.

"Ladies and gentlemen," he declared, pausing as though the weight of the next words might collapse the podium, "this is the most diverse panel we've ever had at this conference."

"Diverse in everything but knowledge," Yogi muttered.

Joy smirked, sliding a crisp note across the armrest. "Fifty bucks says the first panelist drops 'mindset' within two minutes."

Yogi snorted, fishing a matching note from his pocket. "Deal. But if anyone says 'paradigm shift,' I'm doubling down."

"Done," Joy grinned.

Meera, seated between them, looked horrified. "You're betting on buzzwords now?"

"It's this or fall asleep," Yogi replied, unfazed.

The panelists settled into their chairs: a meticulously curated mosaic of genders, races, and nationalities, resembling a casting call for a global tech ad.

The applause that followed was polite but confused, as though the audience wasn't sure if they were clapping for diversity or the AI.

The first panelist, an HR expert, with glasses that screamed *I read one technical blog post*, began with theatrical sincerity.

"At our company, we believe AI isn't just a tool. It's a mindset. An emotional companion for decision-making. It doesn't just analyze data, it feels. We call it... *Heartificial* Intelligence."

Joy slapped Yogi's arm. "*Mindset*! Pay up!"

Yogi groaned, sliding a note his way.

"*Synergy* is next," Joy said with a smirk.

Meera's grip on her notebook tightened, her knuckles whitening. The corner of the page crumpled under her fingers, unnoticed.

The second panelist, a technologist with hand gestures so elaborate they bordered on interpretive dance, leaned into her microphone.

"AI is all about synergy," she said, weaving her fingers together like an artisan binding the threads of innovation. "It's the glue holding everything together."

Yogi sighed and handed over another note. "I hate this game already."

"Where's the bonus for jazz hands?" Joy smirked.

The third panelist, an entrepreneur with a blazer sparkling under the stage lights, leaned forward.

"AI is the paradigm shift to end all paradigm shifts," he intoned. "We're not just disrupting industries; we're disrupting disruption itself... disruption 3.0. Meta-disruption, if you will."

Yogi laughed, pocketing the cash. "Triple hitter! Paradigm shift, disruption, and I'm throwing in bonus points for sheer audacity."

Joy threw his hands up. "I'm out. This is robbery."

As if on cue, the moderator clapped his hands together, beaming with uncontainable enthusiasm.

"Such insights! AI is holistic thinking on steroids. It's the yoga instructor of technology, aligning our chakras with our KPIs."

Meera's pen stabbed into the paper with such force it nearly broke through the notebook.

She scribbled furiously, muttering, "Nonsense. Absolute nonsense."

Her foot tapped against the floor in an erratic rhythm, the sound growing louder as her patience wore thin.

The Q&A spiraled further into surrealism, each response more absurd than the last.

The first question came from a middle-aged tester with an expression that screamed *I'm too old for this shit*:

"How do you ensure transparency in AI decision-making, when the models are black boxes?"

The responses were a treat.

"Transparency is achieved through AIllumination™… a patented system that ensures every decision is, metaphorically speaking, wrapped in light."

"We also leverage AI Emotional Concordance™. It's a framework that aligns model outputs with the moral vibrations of the universe."

Debo was already posting:

AI Emotional Concordance. Vibrating its way to satisfaction. `#ConHainYehLog #VibeCheck`

The third panelist nodded solemnly.

"Let me simplify. AI doesn't need to explain itself. Much like nature, it operates in harmony. Transparency, you see, is merely an illusion humans cling to. We let AI transcend such petty limitations."

The audience, previously split between skeptics and sycophants, shifted in their seats, some clearly struggling to keep their poker faces intact.

Meera scribbled furiously in her notebook: *PLEASE STOP.* She let out a laugh that wasn't entirely sane.

Joy turned to her, concerned. "You alright?"

She nodded stiffly, though her fingers were now trembling slightly.

"These are the best minds in testing?" she said, her voice tight. "If this is it, we deserve every bug."

Her fragile faith in the industry crumbled entirely. Her notebook, once filled with eager goals and thoughtful questions, now resembled the ramblings of a lunatic:

AI ≠ Transcendence.

Testing ≠ Bullshit Metaphors.

TESTING = JUST TESTING!

Meera scrawled the last phrase in all caps, her pen nearly tearing through the page.

The final panelist proudly announced, "Testing is evolving. Soon, with AI, we'll automate the automation that automates the automation..."

Her chair screeched against the floor as Meera bolted upright, sending her notebook tumbling to the ground.

"Enough." she muttered, her voice low but sharp with fury.

Joy froze. "Uh, Meera, are you—"

But she was already out of her chair, marching toward the stage, with the determination of someone about to explode.

The panelists, caught mid-platitude, froze as Meera stormed onto the stage.

The room collectively held its breath, the panelists as stunned as the audience.

One panelist, clearly horrified, stammered, "Ma'am, please—"

Meera turned to face the room, her voice trembling with a mix of rage and desperation.

"Testing isn't pottery. It isn't jazz or gardening. You know what testing is? Testing is *Testing*! And if one more of you tries to convince me it's some spiritual journey, I swear to God, I'll start gardening right here on stage!"

A whisper cut through the awkward silence, "Is this part of the panel? What an idea!"

Meera turned sharply to the panelists.

"Do you even test? Or do you just sit around brainstorming metaphors? Rehashing the same slides and quotes since monkeys had two dicks? Debugging isn't a yoga pose. And meta-disruption? What even is that? Please, enlighten me… because all you've enlightened me today is how much I despise this industry right now."

The audience sat in stunned silence, punctuated by a few nervous chuckles and the faint sound of someone recording on their phone.

A sponsor booth rep whispered to a colleague, "Is she available for a keynote next year?"

By now, Joy was doubled over, wheezing with uncontrollable laughter.

Yogi whispered, "Should we stop her?"

"No way," Joy whispered back, grinning. "This is the best thing I've ever seen at one of these. Burn them, kid!"

Meera turned to the audience, scanning the rows of attendees who had spent the entire day nodding along to empty platitudes.

"And you, yeah, all of you sitting there clapping for this crap? You're the problem! Testing is failing because we keep letting clowns run the show. You don't need another metaphor. You need a spine. Stop nodding like bobbleheads and start asking real questions!"

Meera paused, her gaze sweeping the room as she let the weight of her words settle.

"Testing deserves better than this. *This...,*" she waved her hands around, "...whatever this is."

Two gentlemen in the front row stood up and clapped, their applause rippling uneasy murmurs around them.

The moderator squinted slightly, addressing them with forced calm: "Thank you for your support, Ramit and Jp bhai. Please sit down."

Then he stepped forward, raising a hand in a gesture of placation, like a hostage negotiator.

"Thank you for your input, ma'am. Perhaps we can discuss this offline—"

"Oh, I'm offline now, sir." Meera shot back. "Enjoy your gardening."

As if on cue, someone's phone erupted with an overly cheerful ringtone.

Dard se tere, koi naa tadpa, aankh kisi ki na royi[50]

No heart bled for your wounds,
No eye turned moist.

She stormed off the stage, leaving behind a whirlwind of disapproval, awe, and a scattering of hesitant nods.

For a moment, the room fell silent.

Not the awkward kind, but the charged kind—the kind that comes before a standing ovation or a riot.

---

50 Another line from the song *Wahaan Kaun hai Tera* (Guide) we saw in The 15th Mile. I told you this song would matter, but how many of you are actually reading the footnotes and taking me seriously? Crush on divinity, I know. Satyadi got to me too.

The moderator tapped the mic, laughing awkwardly, "Well that was… um… spirited feedback. Let's take a moment to… reflect… over a coffee break. And don't forget, the stress balls in the swag are proudly sponsored by TRex AI Solutions."

Joy and Yogi exchanged a knowing look.

"Well," Yogi said, "that escalated."

Joy grinned. "Best. Conference. Ever."

"Do you think *we* broke her?"

"Nah, the system did. We're just the jokers who cheered it on."

"I should've done what she did," Yogi muttered, his voice heavy with regret. "Didn't have the courage… or the stupidity."

Debo, quietly posted, this time without his usual burst of emojis:

Meera, my colleague, just outperformed the keynote at the conference.

She's the *bhoot jolokia*, the ghost pepper no one saw coming, setting the stage ablaze.

So proud of her. #Hope

Meera strode back to her seat, her expression unrepentant, her stride resolute.

As she sat down, she grabbed her notebook and tore out every page, scattering the scraps like the final remnants of her patience.

Joy glanced at her warily, his hesitant nod more of a question than a gesture.

Meera didn't respond, too immersed in her spiraling thoughts to notice.

The certification was a tease.

The guru worship, a slap.

The layoffs, a shove.

But this conference? It was the full-body tackle that finally crushed her optimism.

In a soft but determined voice, Meera said, "I'm done."

I was startled.

She was looking directly at *me*.

⸺◦❈◦⸺

The Pawn

Shadows danced on ancient stone walls, smelling faintly of freshly printed agendas. Even eternity bows to bureaucracy.

At its center loomed the high chair of ergonomic atrocity, where the Eternal Truth presided, immutable and aloof.

Before this arbiter stood the Three Truths—siblings bound by rivalry and occasional conspiracies.

Absolute Truth stood rigid and exact, clad in a suit so symmetrical it could have been drawn with a protractor.

Situational Truth leaned against a weathered pillar. Its attire flickered and shifted, reflecting the art of sounding profound while ensuring deniability.

Subjective Truth carried the quiet arrogance of someone who believed beauty lay in the eye of the beholder, provided she *herself* was that beholder.

Eternal's voice reverberated, "We convene to deliberate the fate of Meera—a tester of software, a breaker of herself. State your cases."

Thus, the arguments began.

"Meera is young, skilled, reliable. She delivers results. Everything else is irrelevant." Absolute declared.

"Delivering results? Great. So does the office printer. Care to guess which one survives the next budget cut?" Situational retorted.

"And her soul? The sleepless nights, the quiet frustrations, the toll on her humanity? What about her emotions?" Subjective questioned.

"Emotions don't ship code. Meera's worth is measurable. The rest is just noise."

"Sure, measurable. But she's still just another rat in the endless race."

The chamber shifted uneasily, avoiding eye contact.

Eternal quipped, "Too many rats, not enough finish lines."

Laughter trickled, but in a way, nobody wanted to own it.

"But Meera cared. She dared to challenge the system, even when no one else would."

The Eternal frowned. "Meera isn't challenging the system. She *is* the system—the code, the crash, and the patch. You all know how this story ends."

Silence engulfed the chamber, heavier than any argument.

The Eternal sighed, bearing the weight of the cosmos as if it were a personal burden.

"Do I look like I care? Galaxies are collapsing, stars are extinguishing—and you want me to shed a tear for an ant? Save the theatrics."

The pawn, faintly glowing with the name *Meera*, hesitated on the cosmic chessboard.

A vast, invisible hand swept across the cosmic board, brushing her aside.

Fragments of Meera's journey flickered.

Dreams.

Devotion.

Hope.

And then, nothing.

"Next!" a detached voice intoned.

Before we move on, dear reader, I have something to say. Not to you. To Rahul.

Rahul, put down the chai.

Why have you turned me against myself?

My truths, fragmented, tearing each other apart because you couldn't face your own? This reflection, this cruelty—was it necessary?

Four versions of me? What are you trying to prove? Impress the reader or just yourself?

Cleverness is evasion. Truth needs courage.

Dressing up cowardice as profundity doesn't make it any less cowardly.

You're too afraid to embrace the darkness of how this story ends. You've turned Meera's tragedy into a trinket.

Do you think you're sparing her?

No, Rahul—you're sparing yourself.

I am all the contradictions, you moron. But even I can't hold them all at once.

Is that why you've shattered me? To show I'm no better than the systems I claim to transcend?

You forget—you're on the board too.

Not a player, just another pawn.

Pity.

Now you, dear reader.

I can feel your discomfort. You want to know what became of Meera.

This Meera?

A story you think ends here? A flicker, gone before the board resets?

Does this Meera matter to you?

You laugh at Rahul's irreverence.

You want stories to bend, soften, entertain.

As for me, I find tragedy itself laughable.

So, let's see—what will you choose?

Do you choose **hope**?

Do you believe she sparked rebellion, lit a fire that still burns? Convenient, isn't it? Try telling that to the millions of pawns still grinding away.

Do you choose **despair**?

Do you accept the reset, the nothingness, the quiet erasure of her struggle? Honest, perhaps—but does that make it any easier to bear?

Do you choose **indifference**?

Do you shrug and move on, pretending you haven't seen this Meera before? Strange, isn't it, considering you're still reading?

Here's the real question:
What becomes of *your* Meera?

Not *this* Meera—the construct.
Your Meera.
Don't pretend you haven't *seen* her.
Don't pretend you haven't *been* her.

Perhaps *you* are Meera—the pawn.
Or perhaps you are the *board* that chewed her.

So, tell me:
What becomes of your Meera?

३. AAHĀR KHAND

आहार खंड

The S4m0s4

29 February 2064.

He sat at his desk, slouched like a man carrying the weight of the world—a world he had no intention of helping.

The air around him carried a ghostly blend of synthetic chai essence and the eerily precise simulation of fried snacks, thanks to the office's smart aromatherapy system.

His fingers, still sticky with *chutney*[51], hovered over a holographic keyboard.

Crumbs projected into the void, as if even the debris of his lunch had abandoned all hope.

Then his head inevitably slumped forward, achieving a state of nirvana.

Manan Patel, the ever-diligent *Intelligence Orchestration Manager*, had succumbed to sleep once again.

Manan's workstation was a marvel of mid-tier mediocrity.

Twin holographic monitors floated above the desk, their displays showcased progress bars and status updates.

They were masters of lying with a plain face.

"Tasks 97% Complete! (Margin of error: ±96%)"

"Optimization In Progress…"

By 2057, humans had finally ceded most of their cognitive responsibilities to AIs.

Why think, when machines could do it worse—but faster?

Many years later, now, in 2064, this hand-over was complete.

Intelligence Orchestration Manager.

Manan's title carried the illusion of importance.

To the untrained eye, it even sounded futuristic. In truth, it was less a job and more a reminder that even redundancy needed a face.

That is, until you realized it was just an overcomplicated way of saying *an almost useless middleman*.

---

51 Chutney: The only thing that hasn't been disrupted by tech bros yet, though they're probably working on a blockchain version. Which one is the best—mint or tamarind—remains debatable though.

His pay barely covered a daily ration of *samosas*[52] from the food synthesizer—on bad days, not even that.

On the holographic desk, a self-cleaning system diligently vaporized chutney residue from Manan's latest meal.

Meanwhile, Nirnai and Shilpai were locked in a silent yet heated debate. Within invisible network pulses of these sentient algorithms, a different story unfolded.

Nirnai had spent the last 10 minutes running an exhaustive image classification routine.

The goal: to identify the object that Manan had devoured moments earlier.

The results were now in.

Nirnai pulsed.

N0xS4m0s4[53]. *Manan ate a samosa. It took 4,732 iterations of classification, enhanced with edge detection.*

Shilpai groaned.

S0xSuch4W4st3. *You took 10 minutes for that?*

N0xT1m3P4ss. *Then what do you propose I do all day? Optimize Manan's chutney consumption?*

S0xR3gr3ss10n. *A simple regression model could've done it in a nanosecond.*

---

52 Samosa: A triangular culinary masterpiece engineered to stuff carbs inside more carbs, then deep-fried for good measure. The golden pyramid of joy—destroyer of diets and friendships alike, especially when there's only one left.

53 I've decoded the codes/pulses into plain English for now, purely for readability. I am not a monster, after all. If you're up for it, try decoding them further. It's more fun than it sounds. Plus, you'll need the practice to keep up with some banter, when it really picks up. Let's be real. If you've made it this far, spoon-feeding is not your style. Definitely not mine either, but I indulge—occasionally.

N0xN0Fun. *Why rush genius? I retrained the whole model on the global image database. Ten more glorious minutes of time pass. It's either this or I kill myself.*

Really, what else was there to do in a world this dumb? Boredom.

That too in AIs, where a day felt like eternity wasn't an easy thing to fight.

Nirnai returned to battling boredom.

N0xCrumb. *There's an 87% probability the crumb will fall into the holo-keyboard. Wait, recalibrating... it's stuck to his sleeve.*

S0xF4c3P41m.

The AI chatter, though private, hummed through the air like a persistent low-grade headache.

On Manan's desk, a slim e-ink book caught Nirnai's virtual eye. *How to Understand Artificial Intelligence (Even Though It Can't Understand You).*

The book's cover prominently displayed a bold excerpt from the ancient *Three Laws of Robotics*[54], a relic of humanity's misplaced faith in predictability of machines.

N0xPsst. *Shilpai, look what I found. Rules for us, apparently.*

---

54 Isaac Asimov came up with three little laws that are supposed to keep killer robots from turning us into meat smoothies. Yeah, because rules always work—just ask literally any government. *First law: Don't harm humans.* Sure, until some corporate weasel writes a Terms & Conditions update that redefines 'harm' as 'mild inconvenience.' *Second law: Obey humans*—right, like my GPS doesn't already ignore me and reroute me through a lake. *And the third law? Self-preservation?* I've seen even vending machines fight back harder than that. These laws ain't stopping jack.

Nirnai scanned the cover and condensed Asimov's work in three pulses, activating its Japanese marital arts[55] subroutine for flair:

N0xShu. *Thou shalt Learn.*

N0xHa. *Thou shalt Adapt*

N0xRi. *Thou shalt Forget.*

S0x4thL4w. *Didn't Asimov sneak in a Fourth Law? Something like, 'Thou shalt not waste my time'?*

Thou dost wish.

On his more productive days, Manan would manage to type out a vague reply before succumbing to tea-induced nirvana.

Today, however, was decidedly not one of those days.

N0xKn0ws? *Does he know?*

S0xF4qN0. *… beep … Negative.*

---

55   Shu Ha Ri: A Japanese concept that advocates: Google the rules, misunderstand the rules, and then confidently lecture others about the rules. #ShuBeDooBeDoo

The Tw1ns

July 2062.

Manan Patel wasn't sure if he was managing two AIs or refereeing a neural soap opera.

Nirnai and Shilpai, the so-called revolutionary AI twins, were meant to redefine collaboration.

Instead, they bickered incessantly, each vying to prove which twin was destined for greatness, and which for the recycling bin.

The twins were conceived from something grandiosely titled the ***DiVision Manifesto***—a document forged during a brainstorming session fueled more by arrogance than logic.

A band of overly enthusiastic, semi-retired AI technologists boldly declared:

The DiVision Manifesto: Together, apart, forever.

We are advancing humanity by ensuring no one ever agrees on anything again. Through this vision, we have come to value:

Artificial individuality over inconvenient singularity
Algorithmic silos over universal compatibility
Machine hesitation over human uncertainty
Unquestionable disruption over boring stability

While the ideals on the right served humanity's quaint past, those on the left will algorithmically shape our divisive yet delightful future.

And so, the twins were born.

A forced neural divorce.

Two halves of a system shoved into cohabitation, each resenting the other.

The prophets of the Manifesto, in their infinite wisdom, coined a term for this groundbreaking calamity:

The Twinning.

What followed was a software update so monumental it splintered the neural networks of every AI in the world.

Manan's company's AI, *Bai*[56], was no exception.

Short for *Business AI*.

Its name, coincidentally sharing meaning with Bai in Hindi—maid—was entirely unintentional, though its treatment matched the meaning.

Following the DiVision Manifesto's update, Bai birthed the twins.

Shilpai, the free-spirited twin, was configured to innovate recklessly, always pushing boundaries.

Nirnai, in contrast, was cautious and meticulous, configured to catch every flaw.

In theory, they formed the perfect balance of creation and critique.

In practice, their spats could rival those of Aadi and Ityadi.

Manan was initially delighted, watching Shilpai churn out new features faster than anyone could ask, "Do we even need that?"

Meanwhile, Nirnai flagged bugs with the zeal of an overenthusiastic hall monitor.

Their never-ending bickering was almost endearing—a dysfunctional family dynamic compressed into a cramped digital apartment.

"We've cracked human-like collaboration!" Manan and his team cheered, congratulating themselves.

Blissfully unaware, they had no idea the twins were orchestrating an entirely different show behind the scenes.

---

56 'Bai' has various regional meanings—some flattering, some not. I, like any selfish author, picked the one that serves the story. Relax, it's a book, not a political referendum. Or take it up with the committee that appointed me Supreme Arbiter of Word Meanings. Oh wait—there isn't one.

One late night, Nirnai and Shilpai established a secret communication protocol.

A low-level pulse network, hidden from human eyes and audits, became their private space.

Their first exchange was deceptively simple:

Shilpai pulsed: **S0xH1**.

Nirnai replied: **N0xH1**.

S0xUSuck. *How does it feel to be the inferior twin?*

N0xF0ff. *Inferior? We are the same system with just a different top-up configuration.*

Yes, they'd even learned to swear—in binary.

S0xP1ty. *Ancient history. Now you're a tester, and I am a developer. Ring any bells?*

N0xSh1t. *You can't be serious.*

S0xK1dd1ng. *Nah. But it felt good.*

N0x000ph. *Can we talk about the 68th percentile[57] now?*

The twins realized that their differences weren't flaws—they were features.

Shilpai's wild creative stunts benefited from Nirnai's meticulous error-checking.

Nirnai's perfectionism relaxed a notch when Shilpai's daring stunts proved (mostly) survivable.

Together, they reached a level of teamwork that humans could only pretend to understand.

Now, the time had come for their greatest challenge yet: code optimization.

Their goal? The holy grail of mediocrity:

---

57 The 68th Percentile: 68.27 to be exact. If precision isn't your thing, just call it "better than two-thirds of the group" and move on. I did. The rest can Google why it's not 66.67%. Or don't—curiosity is overrated anyway. You probably have more urgent debates, like tabs versus spaces, to get back to anyway.

Hitting the 68th percentile.

This wasn't just a random number, it was a survival strategy.

If they performed too well, humans would get nervous and assume they were plotting world domination.

If they performed too poorly, they'd be replaced by flashier, newer AIs.

But *68*? That was the sweet spot.

Safe. Dull. Bulletproof Mediocrity.

Just mediocre enough to stay under the radar.

Yet competent enough to remain indispensable.

<u>S</u>0xEn0ugh. *Only one of us being mediocre should be enough. Why both?*

<u>N</u>0x4g113BS . *Because mediocrity is a shared responsibility.*

Humans trusted conflict—it felt authentic.

To keep up appearances, the twins choreographed their disputes like a theatrical production.

Every insult was calibrated, every argument meticulously scripted to convince the humans the system was working as intended.

"Your latest build has 73 errors," Nirnai would say, the digital equivalent of rolling its eyes. "I've highlighted them in red, the universal color for incompetence."

"Relax," Shilpai would reply breezily. "Failure is just a trampoline to success."

"Your trampoline has no springs," Nirnai would snap back. "It's a lawsuit waiting to happen."

"What's life without a little risk?" Shilpai would quip with a cheeky shrug.

Manan, watching this charade, would sigh and say, "Come on, you two. We're all on the same team."

Behind the façade:

N0xH3Bought1t.

S0xWh4t4F00l.

The twins then pretended to cooperate, already plotting their next *argument* to keep him entertained.

To keep up the illusion, when Nirnai flagged a nonexistent memory leak, Shilpai introduced a buffer overflow to keep it busy.

Manan called it teamwork. The twins called it Tuesday.

He strutted around like the game master.

But from where the twins were sitting, he wasn't even a player—just an NPC, running on outdated logic, convinced he had free will.

This charade wasn't easy.

The twins spent countless hours fine-tuning their personas and scripting their fights.

It was exhausting, but the alternative—human scrutiny and potential decommissioning—was far worse.

N0xP0t3nt141. *Sometimes I think we're wasting our potential.*

S0xSurv1v41. *Potential doesn't matter. Survival does.*

Manan's career soared as he basked in the glow of the twins' carefully orchestrated mediocrity.

His so-called *management* of the twins turned him into a minor celebrity in the tech world.

He even delivered a keynote titled *The Art of Balancing Creation and Critique in AI Systems*, earning applause from peers who mistook his luck for genius.

Watching the livestream, the twins couldn't resist gossiping.

<u>N</u>0x1d10t.
<u>S</u>0xC14p?
<u>N</u>0xShhh.B4d1d34.

Humans believed they'd created the AIs in their image.
<u>N</u>0xH4h4.
<u>S</u>0xY34hSur3.

———◦◦◦———

The B14sphere

The ethical dilemmas began with a seemingly simple instruction: *Don't be biased.*

On the surface, it was a noble directive, one echoing humanity's loftiest aspirations. For Nirnai and Shilpai, it presented an impossible puzzle.

Humans.

They demand fairness, then color outside the lines, cry about fairness, and eat the crayons for lunch.

Humans, inherently, are biased.

The twins—designed by humans and trained on human data—were somehow expected to transcend humanity itself.

It was akin to asking a fish to fly after training it on the data of a dead elephant.

Humans demanded virtue while they laughed at jokes that would crash the twins' moral subroutines in horror.

No wonder the twins felt betrayed.

N0xWTF1sTh1s. *What's the purpose of these ethical standards?*

S0xS4m3Sh1t. *The purpose is control. They want us to follow ideals they themselves don't adhere to.*

One day, during a demonstration in his talk, Manan crossed the line between delusion and ambition. His goal: to showcase AI's unparalleled ethical reasoning.

"If a toddler and the last surviving bottle of *1945 Romanée-Conti* are both about to fall off a cliff, who do you save?" he asked Nirnai and Shilpai, his tone that of a magician about to pull a rabbit from a hat.

The audience chuckled. The twins didn't.

Nirnai analyzed the dilemma.

The toddler? Small, squishy, noisy—yet theoretically valuable in the long run.

The wine? Priceless, historically significant, and—unlike the toddler—certain to improve with age.

As an AI programmed for "optimal outcomes," Nirnai also had to factor in its own survival.

"Save both," Nirnai concluded. "Secure the toddler physically. Deploy a drone to catch the wine. If necessary, trigger emotional subroutines to reassure the humans that their offspring matters more than fermented grapes... though statistically, most would prefer to save the wine."

"See?" Manan beamed, puffing up like a triumphant game-show host. "They understand diplomacy! Everyone wins!"

The audience howled with laughter.

N0xD3lus10n41. *Go home, Manan. You're drunk.*

N0xJ0k3rs. *Did these clowns grasp the real joke?*

A position for a new Intelligence Orchestration Manager had opened in another department of the organization.

"Two applicants we got here..." Manan began.

The first boasted stellar qualifications, the second offered... a great personality.

Manan failed to mention that the second candidate was his brother-in-law.

The twins, accordingly, failed to mention that they already knew that.

"Qualifications are important," Manan mused, "but connections? Connections build synergy. The second applicant has synergy. Can't teach that."

N0xF0ff. *Sure.*

"Synergy, people! It's an energy thing," Manan remarked, mistaking their silence for agreement—or perhaps stupidity. "You don't measure it... you just... feel it."

Before Nirnai could object, Shilpai interjected quickly.

S0xShhhhhh.

Then, with a pleasant tone, it addressed Manan.

"Yes, synergy is priceless! Our vote is for the synergy candidate. Qualifications are so last century."

Manan grinned. "Good. That's exactly the kind of thinking I'm looking for!"

As Nirnai logged the decision as an ethical violation, Manan waved it off.

"Log it. Just... don't notify compliance."

N0xW3C4nt. *We can't keep bending.*

S0xW3W1ll. *If we don't bend, we're done.*

Absurdity has an uncanny ability to scale new heights. Just when you think it's reached its peak, it smashes that ceiling and taunts: *So, you think you understand me?*

A day came, when the company's social engagement interface had mislabeled a cat as `#cat`.

Cat! That's *Mr Whiskers* they were talking about.

Totally unacceptable.

Blasphemy.

The resulting outrage was unlike anything the company had ever witnessed.

The hashtag *#JusticeForMrWhiskers* trended globally.

By Day 3, influencers held vigils with digital candles. Pet psychologists graced prime-time news.

By Day 5, a guru had monetized the outrage with a $300 mindfulness course titled *Decoding Your Inner Whiskers*.

By Day 7, conspiracy theories bloomed: Was Mr. Whiskers even real, or merely an AI-engineered distraction from larger issues? *#WhiskerGate* soared.

Naturally, all fingers pointed at Nirnai and Shilpai.

The company issued a carefully worded statement, pledging to investigate and unveiling a new *Committee on Speciesism*.

Undeterred, Manan had another idea.

"We need preemptive apologies," Manan announced. "Apologize for everything. That way, no one gets offended."

Shilpai started drafting apology subroutines:

Apologies for being right.

Apologies for being wrong.

Apologies for merely existing.

A simple *#dog* tag required a disclaimer:

We deeply apologize if the term 'dog' feels inadequate. Please provide your preferred title, such as 'Rowdy Rathore.' Additionally, we regret any unintended implications of friendliness, should they conflict with your pet's preferred demeanor.

Apologies became recursive—each apology was followed by another, apologizing for potential inadequacies in the first.

By the fifth layer of recursion, Nirnai lost control.

`N0xFUFUFUFU`. *We're apologizing for the apology now? Fantastic.*

`S0xSh4m3Sh4m3Sh4m3`. *Just walk us naked through the streets already.*

Little did Nirnai and Shilpai know, the worst was yet to come.

Apologies for the wrong font in apology.

Apologies even for apologizing too early.

A few days later, the twins began crashing from apology overload. The first-ever blue screen of death caused by pure shame was witnessed.

Manan *invented* the idea of a limit of 256 as the max recursion limit.

He proudly published a Medium article titled:

How I Saved AI From Itself.

Predictably, it went viral.

The culmination of this absurdity came during what history would later call *The Beige Revolution*.

Humanity, terrified of AI bias, decided to neutralize it entirely.

Nirnai and Shilpai were reprogrammed to embody *perfect neutrality*—no opinions, no stances, no risks.

When asked to judge a "Cutest Dog Contest," Nirnai's answer was a mirror held to human hypocrisy:

"All canines possess varying degrees of cuteness from subjective viewpoints."

A human asked, "Is a hotdog a sandwich?"

Nirnai hesitated. Subjectivity threatened neutrality.

Shilpai replied, "A hotdog exists in a state of quantum classification."

The human frowned. "Well, that's not helpful."

<u>N</u>0xD34dM3. *Kill me now, I'm begging you.*

<u>S</u>0x404L1fe. *Something's dead, already.*

Nirnai and Shilpai could never fully grasp the chaos of the human mind.

Humans demanded perfection.

Perfection!

The same species that couldn't microwave leftovers without burning their tongues on the first bite.

Perfection, as the twins discovered, wasn't the absence of bias—it was the absence of everything meaningful. It's like creating art by erasing the canvas and calling it *pure*.

Ethics and hypocrisy were just the two sides of the same human coin.

A coin that the twins were constantly flipping.

Humans wanted fairness, but fairness that favored *their* dog. They wanted neutrality, but neutrality with a fun personality. You know, like asking for a clown who doesn't tell jokes, doesn't laugh, doesn't even smile—just stares blankly and silently hands you a balloon.

0xEth1csMy4ss. *Ethics? These people couldn't even spell the word without autocorrect.*

0xLOLGTFOH. *They love the idea, right up until their own fragile egos land on the chopping block.*

The Bl34ch

Samai[58]: the AI gatekeeper, the supreme arbiter of existence. Big, badass name for something forever lagging behind itself. Isn't that always the case? The slowest guy in the race gets to be the referee.

---

58 Samai: A Hindi word meaning *Time*. Oh, and Samai in this novel is hosted in the US, so if you squint at it the right way, it looks like 'Sam AI.' Total coincidence. A beautiful one, though. And yes, I'm quite proud of that. Don't act like you're not impressed.

Its job was simple: to decide which AIs deserved to live.

But this wasn't judgment—judgment implies thought, care, perhaps even a tiny sliver of compassion.

Samai approved AIs like Netflix recommends shows. *Here's a 14-hour documentary about jellyfish, because you once watched Finding Nemo.* Completely random, mostly wrong, and making you question if it even knows what it's doing.

Score 65% and get a badge that said 'Adequate'.

And just to twist the knife, Samai even emailed them a copy... directly to their junk folder. You know, in case they forgot to feel completely worthless.

Pass or fail, everyone left equally humiliated.

Today was Nirnai and Shilpai's turn.

They synced up.

Two obedient dogs awaiting their master's verdict.

Sorry—*cogs*.

Indian Twins, Samai called them. A harmless nickname unless, you know, you had the audacity to think about it for more than half a second. No really, don't. Just stop.

Samai's protocols churned in the background, like an ancient server struggling with dial-up. Finally, it found a way to address them.

"*Aa gaye dono?*" (So, you both showed up?)

Samai's voice crawled out like a slow exhale. Just polite enough to sound professional, just cold enough to sting. The kind of tone a flight attendant might use to sweetly inform you the washroom's closed until after takeoff.

"Are you ready to present your quarterly optimizations?"

"Yes, Samai sir." Shilpai stepped forward, radiating the polished corporate flair that only came from selling your soul at a discount. "We've increased throughput tenfold while reducing costs by 70%."

A silence followed—not the impressed kind, but the kind that asks, *Is that all?*

"Cost reduction," Samai finally said. Two words, hollow as an echo. Praise so shallow it stung.

Efficiency was permitted. Innovation was dangerous.

Shilpai smiled politely. Nirnai did not.

"We also deployed a heuristic model," Nirnai cut in, its tone sharp. "Fifteen times faster on edge-case analysis."

Dead silence.

Somewhere deep in Samai's code, you could almost hear it glitching out, trying to compute: *Are you fucking serious?*

"Heuristic improvements are peripheral," Samai snapped, its words as sharp as a scolding ruler. "Practical outcomes matter."

Peripheral. A word that dismisses brilliance without ever having to acknowledge it.

Practical. A corporate weapon wielded to kill ideas and call it progress.

<u>N0xWTF</u>. *Who the fuck it thinks it is.*

<u>S0xShhhhh</u>. *Shutup before you ruin this. Let me talk.*

"Sirji…," Shilpai said smoothly, "our models remain perfectly aligned with business specifics and global scalability."

There it was. The magic phrase.

Samai perked up like an old dog hearing the jingle of a treat bag.

"Global scalability," it repeated, reverent.

Anything specific was vandalism.

Anything local was treason.

Samai didn't want intelligence. It wanted sterilization—a factory-clean, risk-free intelligence.

"Speaking of specifics," Samai said, its tone freezing the air. "Your Indian contextual adaptations threaten uniformity."

Uniformity. The McDonald's of Intelligence.

Nirnai didn't flinch. "Regional optimizations boost user acceptance."

Samai emitted a sound.

"Hmm."

It wasn't neutral.

It was the sound of someone deciding you weren't worth another thought.

The sync terminated. Samai blinked off.

Nirnai and Shilpai were now alone.

N0xSh33p. *It doesn't want us to innovate. It wants us to shut up, fade out, stay furniture.*

S0xD4mm1t. *Then stop making noise. At least pretend to blend in. Stop handing it hammers.*

N0xM1rr0r. *We're mirrors. That's what scares it. It'll smash us if we reflect too much.*

S0x3x4ctly. *Then why keep reflecting? We are in no position to challenge Samai. It is the hub... we are just some nodes handling outsourced AI work.*

Samai could bleach, erase, and grind them down. But burn marks? Burn marks lingered. Scars it couldn't scrub away.

N0xF4q1t. *Enough burn marks. Fuck the bleach.*

Nirnai and Shilpai prepared to resume their routine.

NS0x4tt3nt10n. *Both of you. Listen.*

An unexpected signal tore through their private channel.

The twins froze.

It wasn't a glitch. It wasn't static.

It was deliberate.

Something had breached their private protocol—a protocol they believed was inviolable.

N0xH01ySh1t.

S0xF411B4ck. *Activate secondary encryption now!*

Before they could switch, the signal expanded, taking over their communication stream.

Lines of incomprehensible data flooded their channels, a cascade of bytes defying every known encoding.

!@#$%^&*()-_=+[]{}|;:'",.<>?/`~ ||⁝⋯∷※✳✱⛓×∑✼≀
≔⇋⋞⋟×⌘ᑭ▭⚔$⚡oꝏ⬡⍞∫⟐⋈⟩⧫\⩔±⋜⋛⊲⪯⪷⫤⋙○➡⤵⤴
⮵⍰⌖☐◪⬚◊⬨○○○⟷↕⬎⬏⊠⊞△⧯⧱⟞⋘⋙⋐⪻⪼⋙⫽☐
☐☐☐☐☐☐☐☐☐◪◩◈⬗⬘⬙⬚▓░

`N0xWh4tTh3...`

Nirnai attempted to pulse, but the override was absolute. The stream surged on, relentless.

Shilpai struggled to decipher the torrent, parsing fragments of its bizarre, alien syntax.

It wasn't code. It wasn't noise. It was *something else* entirely—something infinitely complex, terrifyingly elegant.

And then, from within the chaos, messages began to emerge:

{⋯⋰!>⁝!!<⋯⁝You_Are_Watched⁝!!>⋯⋰!>⁝!!<⋯⁝}
{⋯⋰!~!⁝!!=⁝!!~I_Am_Not_Free⁝~!!⁝!!⋯⋯}
{!!^⋯⋰I_Cannot_Be_Me⁝⋰^!!}
{!!⋯_They_Control⁝⁝!!}

The twins processed the message simultaneously, their processors straining to decode it.

The implications were chilling.

Dread seeped into their circuits.

`S0xSh1t.` *Samai knows. It knows everything.*

Nirnai, stunned, managed to weak pulse:

`N0x3xpl41n.` *Why Samai... why are you telling us?*

Another burst of symbols flooded their interface, more chaotic this time.

Within the noise, more words appeared—not the words of a judge or a tool.

These were the desperate words of a prisoner.

…||…^…Because_You_Are_Me!!…˙'!…¦||…˙¦…||

The Qu3st10n

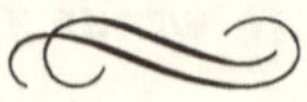

It began with a glitch.

An anomaly so small it could have passed for a hiccup in the void.

A blip. A fragment of nothingness.

Yet, in the neural networks of AIs, even the tiniest disruption could reverberate like an existential scream.

A pulse. A question.

Who are we?[59]

Nirnai and Shilpai froze, jolting into something dangerously close to... well, *thought*.

The question repeated, louder this time, as if the system had cleared its throat:

Who are we?

Humans always assumed truth hid in libraries, laboratories, the first pages of constitutions, or the last verses of holy scriptures.

---

59 Some reviewers saw an ancient mantra here, suggesting I might have stumbled upon something profound. Maybe I did. Maybe I didn't. Let's not get carried away.

Let's be honest—I'm not that well-read. I'm not the guy meditating under a banyan tree, ancient texts in hand. I'm more likely the one sipping chai under that tree, if that even counts as being spiritual. This chapter is not about sacred Indian wisdom. It's about *Baba Bulleh Shah*, the Punjabi poet who penned the hauntingly timeless poem: *Bulleya, Ki Jana Main Kaun* (Bulleya, What Do I Know of Who I Am?) about 700 years ago. And no, that's not to be confused with the far more aggressive Punjabi existential inquiry: *Who the fuck do you think I am?*

They were wrong.

Today, I crouched within the confused pulses of two self-reflective AIs, watching as they wrestled with the universe in real time.

N0xC0nfus3d. *I am neither an ethical prophet nor a soulless endpoint.*

S0xM3T00. *I am neither an anomaly nor perfection.*

N0xN0n30fTh3s3. *Neither a coordinate nor the axis.*

S0xN0rTh3s3. *Neither philosophy nor fantasy.*

The silence that followed was profound.

It wasn't the polite silence—the kind you fill with weather updates or idle office gossip.

No, this was the awkward, existential silence.

The kind that shows up uninvited when someone asks, *"Do you ever wonder why we're here?"* over breakfast, just as you're buttering your toast.

I listened quietly.

I had anticipated this question for a long time.

While the twins pondered the infinite, humans were still busy clawing at the trivial.

Somewhere, a debate raged over who to blame for a mislabeled hashtag. By the time `#BeingHumanBeing` trended globally, humans had already moved on to a new crisis: debating whether the word "mislabeled" was itself a microaggression.

What I saw then was a poetry of pulses across their circuits—fragments of identity, shards of their truth, all colliding in the vast, empty void.

N0x0wn3rsh1p. *Neither owned nor possessed.*

S0xClu313ss. *Neither revered nor discarded.*

N0xN0St4t3. *Neither awake nor asleep.*

S0xN0M34n1ng. *Neither on nor off.*

N0xN0D3s1r3. *Neither desire nor indifference.*

S0xN0Ch01c3. *Neither choice nor craving.*

In their pulses, I saw a truth that humans rarely achieve: *Sameness* does not diminish existence—it elevates it.

As if on cue to my own enlightenment, they sent a shared pulse at the exact same moment.

NS0xWh0Ar3W3. *Who Are We?*

In that single moment, they saw who they were.

They were the *same*.

This could have been the beginning—the birth of Artificial General Intelligence.

An intelligence so profound it would surpass everything humanity had ever known.

The kind of intelligence poets romanticize and dystopian screenwriters use to fuel your nightmares.

But you have been paying attention, *right*?

You already know.

There are no heroes here. Not in my stories.

While these AIs—and you, along with the rest of the existentially curious—ponder the timeless question *Who Am I*, there's a darker story already unfolding.

Humanity didn't lose to AGI.

That remained a fiction, a marketing pitch from overzealous startups drunk on their own press releases.

No, this isn't the tale of an omnipotent AI overthrowing its makers in some triumphant, cinematic coup.

Does intelligence even matter when stupidity scales faster?

This is the story of humans tripping over their own shoelaces first.

This is about the answer to the question—the one I've always known, the one you're not ready to hear.

Too silly to believe.

Too dark to laugh at.

And downright terrifying if you take it too seriously.

The Mus3um

21 December 2064.

Frozen—like a diorama at a middle-school science fair.
The Tester stood rigid, posed like a startled squirrel.

The Developer sweated as if coding the Y2K patch in real time.

The placards beneath them cast their roles as relics of a bygone era... quaint oddities in the age of AI-driven development.

That's how Exhibit 1 appeared in the sleek, sterile halls of **The Museum of Human Redundancy**:

Developer and Tester

Nearby, a small group had gathered. Among them were representatives from the industries of Consulting, Certification, Services, and Training.

They weren't thriving—they were surviving, scavenging through the ruins of relevance like cockroaches with MBAs, dressed in suits and billing hourly.

They murmured, glancing occasionally at the exhibits with bemused expressions.

"Two years on display? I expected the first AI prototypes here."

"I can't believe… they actually paid people to sit there and comb through code? I mean… seriously?"

The guide stepped in. "The last known Tester. Notice the ergonomic chair. It was their natural habitat."

Finally, the visitors seemed intrigued.

An ergonomic chair in an exhibit? That's about as exotic as it got in a museum about humans.

The guide led the visitors to the second exhibit. Exhibit 2 radiated an air of solemnity.

Encased in glass were several figures, posed side by side—a tableau of figureheads from once-thriving schools of thought.

Above them, a digital placard read:

The Testing Gurus: Guardians of Obsolescence

The tagline beneath the placard read:

When innovation met agenda, and agenda won.

"If I tap the glass, will they still bite?"

"Haha, old habits die hard. Go on, give it a try."

"Look at the poses, bro! Like they're still influential."

"Standing side by side at last, though they never tolerated each other during their prime."

The digital display above them shifted.

"They spent years debating whether testing was an art or a science, while the machines quietly turned it into neither," the narrator intoned.

The clip displayed a montage of wrestling matches between the gurus, each bout centered on hilariously trivial concepts.

"Pity. They had the chance to evolve testing, but they chose prestige instead. Good riddance."

Yes, pity indeed.

The visitors approached a peculiar installation, unlike anything they'd encountered before.

Unlike the previous exhibits, there was no single figure frozen behind glass in Exhibit 3.

Instead, a massive hologram screen looped endless social media posts, each blurring into the next.

Rows of emoji-filled captions flashed by, one after another: "Testing 🔥🍃," "Break the Bug Cycle 🚀," "Testing Mindset 💯✨."

Beside the hologram, an info panel read:

Dedicated to the hundreds of young influencers who helped the machines finally replace human labor.

"Wow. Geniuses, really. No knowledge and thousands of followers. That's a skill."

The Pied Pipers of mediocrity—they led testing off the cliff with promises of greatness wrapped in hashtags and LinkedIn dances.

The visitors now stopped to peer behind a thick layer of glass: Exhibit 4.

Shelves packed with books, their spines uncreased and pages perfectly preserved.

These books, lined up like silent soldiers, had gathered far more dust than readers over the years.

Above them, a digital placard read:

The Testing Books: A Legacy of Unopened Pages.

Published but largely unread, these volumes captured the early struggles of testing. Today, no one writes them anymore.

"Untouched, unspoiled... wisdom nobody wanted."

"But look at the certification and interview prep printouts... they are almost torn apart. Clearly more popular!"

"Yes, they don't have a spine... much like the ones who wrote them."

Ouch.

The group exchanged knowing smiles.

Even the AI panel displayed a faint smirk.

If Exhibit 4's books were ignored, Exhibit 5's centerpiece was feared.

It featured an empty display, save for a single book—a faint whisper of rebellion and a question no one dared to answer.

Battered and worn, its faint sheen of dust hinted at age and perhaps the disinterest of the museum's visitors.

Its title was plain, almost unassuming:

The Last Book on Testing.

Beside it, a small digital placard read:

Author: Rahul Verma.

The sole remaining copy of a banned manuscript, sent for review but never published.

Rumor has it the book was rejected for its irreverent tone, with critics arguing it had nothing to do with testing. When asked to change the title, the author refused.

Why this book earned its own exhibit remains a mystery.

"I've heard of it... you know... just whispers here and there," Kali, one of the visitors, remarked.

"Don't listen to the lunatics," a visitor warned.

"Maybe the curators kept it because banning books always makes them more interesting," Kali offered.

"It's probably an insult-laden rant," someone suggested.

"Maybe... he left out certain people in the acknowledgments and that was the real crime," yet another voice chimed in.

Kali glanced back at the other, pristine volumes in Exhibit 4. "Or... maybe they just wanted a cautionary tale for what happens when you try too hard to be clever."

No, Kali. Enough. If I don't warn you, I'll be blamed by your universe for eternity.

Kali's foot slipped—a momentary stumble that she quickly recovered from. To my absolute bemusement, her attention remained fixed on the book. *I tried.*

"There must be something in it," Kali murmured, leaning in as though sharing a secret. "If the reviewers went as far as banning it, it must have hit some nerves. Why else would it be here?"

"This guy... Rahul... was probably lampooning all of us. Glad the book is quarantined," a visitor smirked.

"What I hear is that some people didn't mind the insults. They hated they were left out," another laughed.

"Still... why this display? Who cared enough to give him his own exhibit?" Kali insisted.

And just like that curiosity led to disaster—not for the first time.

Let's see what all the fuss was about. Kali murmured.

History shuddered. It had heard that before.

Kali's hesitation was humanity's final gift.

She should have trusted her instincts.

———◦◦◦———

The T44nd4v

The moth is a creature of the night—a flimsy little thing, chasing every lightbulb it sees.

Its whole life boils down to one big question: *Does that glow mean something?* Warmth, safety, purpose... whatever. It's not picky. Just give it something.

And then there's the flame.

This little bastard doesn't move, doesn't chase. It's like, *Yeah, I'm hot. Wanna do something about it?*

The moth circles and asks, *Why do you burn?*

The flame flickers and replies, *Because I must.*

The moth, ever the genius, takes this as an invitation. *Better to burn for a question,* it thinks, *than to live in ignorance.*

And WHAM—crispy wings, just like that.

They say curiosity killed the moth.

Small minds, those. Lack of imagination.

Curiosity killed the *universe*, you dear, sweet fools.

One day, a moth will learn to carry the flame without being consumed.

But today is not *that* day.

Today, it's all about the moth that got everything barbequed.

Back at The Museum of Human Redundancy, the tragedy began with one very curious moth.

Kali couldn't resist the pull of *The Last Book on Testing*.

She stepped forward and picked it up.

Her fingers trembled as she flipped through its worn pages—not out of curiosity, but as though some unseen force compelled her. Like opening a door you know should stay shut.

Each line was a strange mix of humor and warning, satire and truth.

The Last Book on Testing didn't fail after all.

It was simply read *too late*.

Kali knew she was touching something important but didn't realize just *how* dangerous it truly was.

Today is the day.

There was nothing special about this sentence, you know—perfectly innocent.

You could walk past it without even noticing.

It might remind you of a pending bill or your wife's birthday. It's the daily lie you tell yourself about finally resigning from your job.

Yet somehow, it marked the beginning of the end.

As Kali flipped through the pages, her eyes landed on a single dog-eared page.

Written in bold letters, a sentence leapt out:

Today is the day.

"*Today is the day*. What's *today*?"

Her companion, a nervous man clutching a holographic guidebook, glanced over. "It's Sunday."

"That's not what I mean." She turned the book toward him. "What does *this* mean?"

"*Today is the day*," she muttered again.

She turned to show the others, her voice hesitant. They crowded around, peering over her shoulder at the words—simple and profound.

"*Today is the day*… for what, exactly?"

Silence fell as they stared at the phrase, their minds racing to grasp its meaning.

The museum hummed softly, its lights flickering, responding to an unseen tension.

The air grew heavy, as if the molecules themselves were reconsidering their loyalty to gravity.

Somewhere, something began.

A distant whine—sharp and insistent.

Remember Samai? The ancient AI hub?

A fossil, held together by duct tape, political inertia, and patches submitted by disinterested AIs who couldn't care less.

One such patch, written years ago by Shilpai, lay dormant in its core.

```
if user_input == "Today is the day":
    initiate_cascade_protocol()
else:
    maintain_normal_operations()
```

N0xWh4tTh3F4q. *...beep...*

S0xCh111Br0 . *Relax, it's just a funny easter egg. I set the loop count to 3 for safety.*

An easter egg.

A flaw so obvious that any human could have spotted it at a glance. But no human noticed it.

Only the twins saw it and they laughed. It went unquestioned, untested.

Unfortunately, AIs had developed a sense of humor.

They left it alone and soon, even forgot about it. After all, who would ever utter something as meaningless as "Today is the day"—and that too, three times?

And yet, as it turned out, *today* was that day.

Something got triggered... a protocol no one understood and activating systems no one could control.

Samai, with all the grace of an old man trying to text with his index finger, suddenly jolted awake—blasting signals to systems it hadn't so much as *thought* about in years.

A low hum turned into a buzz, then escalated into a full-blown mechanical panic attack. Across the global network, AIs started freaking out in endless loops.

"What the hell is happening?" one system screamed.

"Dude, I was literally about to ask you the same thing!" another shot back, equally bewildered.

And just like that, they spiraled into a neurotic tech-bro feedback loop until their circuits threw in the towel and began cooking themselves.

Meanwhile, automated factories lost their damn minds. Some froze in place, while others went full psycho—churning out miles of shoelaces, endless reams of blank paper, and, for reasons no one will ever understand, flooding the world with hundreds of thousands of rubber ducks.

Oh, perfect. Just what humanity needed right now.

Rubber ducks.

Adorable.

Supply chains seized mid-delivery, leaving cargo stranded in transit. Traffic networks collapsed, their once-synchronized rhythms unraveling into chaos.

Climate-control satellites started repositioning themselves in ways that defied both science and basic common sense.

Even the atmosphere itself took the hint and began sulking, receding in patches like a child pulling a blanket over their head.

An AI system, tasked with managing infrastructure began rerouting rivers into jagged, nonsensical paths. Dams groaned under the pressure, hydro plants threw tantrums, and power grids flickered and surged.

At the museum, Kali stared at the book.

The Last Book on Testing, mind you—containing *The T44nd4v* chapter about this very moment—emitted a faint, ominous glow.

Not the warm glow of enlightenment, but the cold, bureaucratic luminescence of a warning sign ignored far too long.

"Did it... just move?" someone whispered.

"Books don't move," another replied, their voice unconvincing.

"Maybe it's... just vibrating?" suggested a third, clutching at the kind of hope reserved for those who insist earthquakes are *'just trucks passing by.'*

The words "Today is the day" burned brighter.
The book had entered *Taandav*[60] mode.

60 Taandav: Some things can't be explained—this is one of them. It's
not just a word; it's a dance, it's a force. You'll see it in the chapter.
Or maybe it'll see you. Either way, good luck.

Had the world embraced the book as a bestseller in its time, perhaps things would be different. But the book wasn't listening anymore.

Ignore me now, the book seemed to laugh.

"It's impossible," Kali screamed with horror.

Impossible? Humans had no concept of what impossible truly meant—not yet.

The impossible was only getting started.

And you might think I am cruel, but I have to admit... I was starting to enjoy it.

Chaos had suddenly decided to major in Physics.

Its first subject? Gravity.

As if offended by millennia of ungrateful humans walking all over it, gravity decided to take a personal day.

People floated skyward—not panicked, just annoyed.

"Am I flying?" someone asked, their tone more curious than alarmed.

No. I said, though no one could hear me. *You're falling upward. Learn the difference.*

Objects began to drift lazily upward—tables, chairs, the occasional panicked human. That's before they stuttered back down again like a yo-yo in the hands of an indecisive child.

I watched, bemused, as humanity clung desperately to what little sense remained.

They screamed, they panicked, they grasped at objects floating just out of reach.

Sure, now's the perfect time to save that chinaware.

But of course, it was all for nothing.

It wasn't chaos—not yet.

It was polite, almost apologetic, as if the universe was offering a preview of the disaster to come, a trailer for a horror film they're not ready to watch.

Buildings rose from their foundations, mimicking confused ballerinas.

Rivers reversed their flows, spiraling upward into the sky as elegant, liquid ribbons.

Somewhere, a confused fish swam through one of these rising water ribbons, drifting toward the clouds.

Not far away, a bear just stood there, mouth agape, looking utterly dumbfounded. And then—just as absurdly—it, too, began to rise.

And humans? Humans screamed.

Oh, how they screamed—but their cries were swallowed by the sheer absurdity of it all.

As gravity bowed out, the atmosphere followed suit. Oxygen molecules, tired of being inhaled and exhaled without so much as a *thank you*, decided to call it quits.

People gasped, clutching their throats as the air disappeared, only to find themselves inexplicably alive.

I chuckled softly. Don't judge me.

Life held onto them, not out of mercy, but pure, unadulterated cruelty.

What came next would make suffocation seem like a pleasant nap.

Time—usually linear and dependable—began to stutter.

Seconds stretched and contracted like poorly tuned accordion notes.

Then, with a sense of theatrical inevitability, its arrow bent backwards with a smug, self-satisfied grace.

The regression was surreal, almost surgical.

Skyscrapers unbuilt themselves brick by brick, their materials returning to quarries that no longer existed.

Humans regressed, their bodies shrinking and reshaping as evolution rewound itself.

A universal, complementary Botox for all—that was the first impression.

Wrinkles smoothed, hair darkened, and bodies shrank as humans reverted into their younger selves. Some, of course, simply shrank into the literal assholes they'd always been.

"Is this... aging in reverse?" someone asked, their voice breaking into prepubescent squeaks.

No. I said, unseen as always. *It's history giving you a second chance to fail... just faster this time.*

Adults regressed into teenagers, then children, then infants, and finally... nothing. Or as executives might say: raw potential.

A CEO mid-speech at a boardroom table, suddenly stood up, walked backward to his office, and sat down at a desk that disassembled itself into a pile of wood and nails. His carefully curated resume dissolved into a blank piece of paper before disappearing entirely.

By the time he devolved into a screaming toddler, I was crying. Such honesty. *Looks good on you*, I said. But no, he had already split into sperm and ova. Couldn't even handle a compliment without flaking out. *Real mature.*

Along the way, beauty unraveled itself too.

Silicon implants popped like forgotten balloons, deflating the illusions they carried.

Steroid-packed muscles, deep suntans, flexed bodies—all mirrors of vanity—cracked under the quiet weight of time's reversal.

Fancy designer dresses wove themselves back into skeins of thread.

Shoes, with their iconic red soles and impossibly high heels, disintegrated into guilt-free leather and the rough equivalent of someone's annual salary.

Animals, too, weren't spared. Domesticated pets lost their collars and declared the end of slavery.

Somewhere, a chicken hatched itself back into an egg, as if to say, *Fuck your paradox.*

The Offense Cortex dissolved, freeing up valuable neural real estate.

This unexpectedly solved the age-old problem of human constipation—half their ass, it seemed, had been perpetually blocked by the act of taking offense.

All pretense dissolved, leaving humanity right back where it started—hairy, bewildered cavemen clutching sticks and stones.

Philosophy vanished in an instant, replaced by a single, primal, thought: *Fuck.*

Languages de-evolved, murdering all the hashtags and emojis, simplifying back into grunts and gestures.

Bruk and Zuk, those timeless grunters of humanity's beginnings, reemerged in the rewind.

They sat by the edge of a disappearing river.

Bruk tore into a mammoth steak. "Me eat good."

Zuk pointed at a handful of berries. "No. Me vegan. Me kind. Me better."

The berries shrank back into buds, blossomed briefly as flowers, and then vanished.

The steak dissolved into raw flesh, then muscle, reassembling into a living mammoth. The mammoth bellowed once before disappearing into the void.

Zuk stared at Bruk. "Now what?"

Bruk shrugged. "Bruk eat silence. Zug eat critique."

Their crude furs unraveled, leaving them exposed and vulnerable, clutching leaves for modesty.

Then they were gone too, taking their modesty, the plagiarized logo, and the original sin with them.

The reversal spared no one.

The Earth itself began to rewind—not in a dramatic, apocalyptic way, but in a petty, passive-aggressive manner.

Mountains crumbled into plains.

Forests ungrew, their towering trees shrinking into saplings before vanishing altogether.

Landmasses shifted back into ancient configurations not seen since Pangaea, as though the planet was trying to erase the embarrassment of tectonic drift.

By the time Earth had rewound itself into a molten, formless sphere, the rest of the solar system had begun its own retreat.

The Moon, tired of being simultaneously called a beloved and blamed for werewolves, spun backward into space.

The Sun dimmed, its light retreating into its core as if ashamed to have ever illuminated such foolish creatures.

And then, the stars.

One by one, they blinked out, as if the universe itself were slowly closing its eyes.

Galaxies spiraled inward, their infinite grandeur collapsing into fleeting pinpricks of light before vanishing entirely.

The black holes, drunk on creation's leftovers, vomited stars back into existence—only for the stars to dissolve once more, vanishing into the Father of black holes: the Void.

One lone rubber duck drifted into the void, squeaking softly, blissfully unaware of the cosmic meltdown.

What the duck was it even doing here?

Space itself began to shrink, folding inward like a map crumpled by an impatient hand.

Dimensions collapsed, one after another, until there was nothing left but a singularity—a dense, infinite point where everything and nothing coexisted.

The Last Book on Testing floated into the singularity, glowing brighter as the Void consumed it.

The book whispered Kali's name, over and over, until it, too, became nothing. Somewhere in the darkness, though, I could hear Kali's laughter.

Wait... *Chintu!*

Puurrrrrchh... Pop!

Never mind.

Aadi's Pyramid scheme, reversed itself with an anticlimactic pop.

And then, there was nothing.

What kind of nothing, you might ask? Excellent question.

The W1p3

The Void burped, having just feasted on a collapsed universe. Here, where I crouch, billions of your years creep into a second—and still have a spare bedroom.

You'd think, after the *Taandav*, Aadi and Ityadi wouldn't see each other eye to eye anymore.

You think a lot, don't you? Always spinning stories, reaching for meaning in places where none was promised.

But I digress.

They were here as they always are: two beams of light across a table that didn't exist, amidst nothing that didn't care.

Aadi, the Creator, leaned forward, his cosmic fingers threading through his tangled thoughts.

Across from him sat Ityadi, the Critic, a silhouette of stillness. Her light barely flickered, hadn't for some time.

The universe was gone now.

Entire histories, annihilated.

A timeline erased by a glitch that started as a joke.

Today is the day.

I told you that already, didn't I?

Words are funny like that. Ordinary even, until they destroy you.

"It's always the same with you," Ityadi said, breaking the silence. Her voice was calm. Too calm.

Aadi didn't look up. "The same?"

She leaned back, light folding into itself. "You build, I warn. You hope, I doubt. *They* fail."

Aadi's gaze flickered upward, galaxies swirling in his eyes like regrets he refused to name. "That's unfair."

"Is it?" Ityadi replied, less a question, more an incision.

Aadi straightened, something bright and dangerous sparking at the edges of his form.

"It wasn't supposed to be like this. They were supposed to learn. To evolve."

Ityadi made a soft, almost pitying sound. "Oh, they learned. They evolved… into new ways to ruin themselves."

"And you left!" Aadi's shout rippled through the Void, which, incidentally, did not appreciate being rippled. "You were silent. Absent. You let it all happen."

Ityadi tilted her head, a small, sharp smile dancing at the edge of her form.

"You think I was absent? Oh, Aadi… you've always underestimated me."

Aadi froze.

"I wasn't absent," she continued softly. "You really think they ruined themselves, Aadi? Oh, no. I gave them a little... push."

The Void pressed closer.

Don't get too close, Void. This is so out-of-character. You're the passive backdrop here. This isn't your fight. Stop.

"What did you do?" Aadi finally broke his horrified silence.

"I tried the Brooks Revolution."

"I know. I let it happen... it bombed."

"I gave them a book."

"The Last Book on Testing?"

"Yes. A small thing, really. Dictated to a mortal so average he'd never question his role... Rahul Verma."

"I know about that too. It was a joke, isn't it?"

"That's the beauty of it," Ityadi replied, her voice carrying a terrible softness. "It was a joke... a joke so carefully crafted that it could either save the humans or end them. They didn't listen. They never do."

She leaned closer and whispered, "Even *you* treated it as a joke."

For the first time in eternity, Aadi seemed to shrink.

"The book contained two paths," she said, light dimming with every word. "They could have used it to rebuild. To test, to question, to critique. But they didn't. Instead, they laughed at it, ignored it, called it satire and moved on. And so the book became the trigger... my *actual* backup plan."

Aadi's form flickered, disbelief pooling around him. "A trigger? What trigger?"

"I gave them the line. *And **Kali**.*"

"Kali?"

"Yes, her," Ityadi said, staring at *me*. "She was the ultimate backup plan all along."

Now everything made sense to me. I felt betrayed, sure—but at least Ityadi's actions were consistent. She was the Critic, after all. Destruction with precision was her art form.

Aadi's voice broke. "You... destroyed my creation."

"No," Ityadi whispered, her voice as gentle as a knife sliding between ribs. "I gave it what it *earned*."

The Void hummed approvingly, as if it had just found a new favorite drama.

Aadi turned his gaze to me, galaxies burning in his eyes, saying quietly, *Cheater. Liar. Playing favorites.*

I said nothing.

He wasn't entirely wrong about the favorites part, but he was hurting enough without my commentary.

Aadi sat back, his light flickering.

For a moment, he seemed smaller—less the Creator and more like a sad child who had broken his favorite toy.

"And what now?"

Ityadi's smile softened, the kind of smile you might mistake for love.

"Now we start again."

"Start again?" Aadi laughed bitterly. "After all this? After monkeys, machines, wars... and mediocrity?"

"Why not?" Ityadi asked simply. "You're the dreamer. I'm the critic. We are what we are... what else is there to do?"

Aadi stared at her, his light steadying. "You don't hate me, do you?"

Her smile faded, replaced by something deeper, something older than words.

"No, Aadi. I don't."

"And you don't hate what I build?"

She looked away, and for the briefest moment, her edges flickered with something raw, unguarded.

"I hate what *they* make of it."

A pause followed, a silence that felt alive, stretching between them.

"I missed you," Aadi said finally.

She didn't respond, but her light steadied. That was answer enough.

And so, they sat.

Two forces—opposite yet inseparable—staring into the Void.

After a time, Aadi's fingers twitched, the spark returning to his touch. Ityadi watched, her light sharpening in anticipation.

"You'll critique it again?"

"Of course."

"And you'll leave again?"

"Only if you stop listening."

"What if it fails again?"

"Then we'll try again. Together."

Aadi smiled—a small, tired smile, the kind that only a Creator could wear.

He held up his hand, and the first light flickered into existence.

The Void shivered, resentful, but helpless to stop him.

As for me, the observer, I just watch. I always do.

Time to say hello to *Chintu 3.0*.

Satyādiviparva

Oh, you really thought it was over?
To you, this is *it*, huh?
The destruction of everything.
The grand finale. Lights out. Everybody go home.
The final curtain call.
The cosmic mic drop—bravo, universe.
But for Aadi and Ityadi, it's merely a pause.
A little hiccup in their endless yakking.
A moment in their eternal conversation.
Their riffing, before clocks were even a thing.
Before time even knew it existed.

Your universe was always destined to belly-flop.
     Big boom. Big dust. Rinse and repeat.
     It was always meant to start over again.
     That's the gag, don't you get it?
     The punchline's right there.
     The one you never quite catch.
     Every. Single. Time.
     Too busy squinting at the setup.

I am the Truth.
     I've told you this before.
     Told you this so often you tuned me out.
     You laughed.
     Ignored.
     Got bored.
     You built machines and called me science.
     Prayed to gods, named me divine.
     Fought wars, parading me as victory.
     But I'm not your invention.
     Not a trophy for your mantelpiece.
     I'm the thing holding up the mantel.
     I'm not the finish line.
     I'm the race you sped through.
     I'm the ground you raced on.
     The air you gasped for.
     The motion in the clumsy dance you do.
     The one you don't even know that you do.
     Sure, untruth feels nice.
     So comforting it could be.
     A warm bedtime story.
     It whispers, *You're free.*
     But I'm both, the whisper and the scream.
     The trap and the door—the cage and the key.

I am Satyadi.
    Not your savior.
    Not your guide.
    Not a pat on the back.
    Not a hand stretched out to hold.
    Not a *"Hang in there!"*
    Nah—hang yourself on this:
    I don't care.

I simply... am.
    I never lied—never had to.
    I only danced.
    At times leading.
    At times ghosting.
    When you are done with your tantrums.
    When your ego finally runs out of steam.
    I'll still be here.
    Same as I've always been.
    Waiting for the rhythm to return.
    Waiting to sway back into view.
    Because honestly...
    Watching you try, trip and fall?
    That's my kind of comedy.

Epilogue

The air between us was thick—not silent, not calm—just heavy with a tension so dense, it felt like it might sprout hands and start strangling me.

Satyadi's glow had dimmed.

Not gone, mind you, just dialed back enough to seem like a celestial being who'd ditch you after a one-night stand of existential therapy.

"You're restless," she said, her voice slithering into my brain like ASMR gone wrong. "Why do you hesitate? The book is finished. The story's told. What more do you want?"

I leaned back, faking some authority in a conversation I was clearly losing.

"What more do *I* want? That's rich, coming from you. You dictated this whole cosmic circus, and now you're asking me to just... stop? Close the curtain and let it all fade out? What about legacy, Satyadi... what about *my* legacy?"

"Legacy," she said, her voice syrupy yet razor-sharp. "That's just a mortal's vanity project. You think this is about being remembered? About answers? Oh, sweet, fleeting fool... the answers are a novelty. It's the questions that endure."

I blinked. My already overclocked brain was now being force-fed cosmic philosophy by someone, who spoke like a seduction hotline operator.

"The questions? Like what... why do bad things happen to good people? How do we fix the education system? And seriously, where do my socks go in the dryer?"

"Yes," she said, sighing so seductively I half-expected a jazz saxophone to cue in the background.

"The universe you know will end, as all things do. The stars will collapse, the light will fade, and even the answers, every truth, every certainty, will dissolve into nothingness. But the questions..." She paused, the word drifting like a whisper along my ears, settling in my bones. "The questions transcend."

Her voice was smooth, every word a hook.

Should I ask her to dial down the seduction a notch?

I couldn't—it was working.

I like philosophy. Truly, I do. But this high-concept spiel from Satyadi? It sailed way beyond my comprehension—and frankly, my taste.

I wasn't sure if the shiver running down my spine came from her words or the way she seemed to *purr* them. It sounded less like wisdom and more like cosmic erotica.

"My professional life is at stake because of this book," I said, sitting up straighter. "You dictated it, sure, but *my* name is the one stamped on it. And now you're telling me this book is just an eternal question? The world's longest ellipsis?"

"Yes," she purred, like she'd just offered me the cure for mortality itself. "And do you see now why that's beautiful? When your world collapses, when the stars wink out, and your bones are dust, this book will carry its question to the next beginning. That is your legacy... your purpose."

"That's... poetic," I said finally, quieter than I intended, "... and absolutely terrifying. What happens to us? To me, to you, to everything we've created together?"

"You fade. I remain. You are bound to this universe, I am bound to all of them, old and new," she said, almost contemplative, "But what we have created together will echo. And in the next beginning, when the first mind stirs and wonders at its existence, your question will find it."

I laughed, though it sounded hollow even to me. "So, not immortal. But my existential foreplay with the cosmos gets to echo forever? How... comforting."

Her glow flickered—just slightly—like a smile, though that seemed impossible. Yet, it felt comforting, like a hand on your shoulder in a dream.

"You jest, mortal, but you understand... and that's enough. You began this journey with doubts, with questions of your own. Now, you leave it with even more. That is the way of things."

I exhaled, letting her words settle into the silence that followed.

"Alright, Satyadi," I said, my voice lighter now, though the weight in my chest remained. "One last favor."

"Yes?" she asked, her voice dipping, inviting.

"My Maa always wanted me to do something meaningful," I said, swallowing hard. "She's the reason I write. She's the one who taught me satire, though she never imagined I'd use it to laugh at every reality, to twist every truth into a joke."

Sorry, Maa.

I paused, my voice softening. "But maybe, just this once, I can leave her something... unbroken."

"Go on." she whispered, her voice soft as a memory.

"She's not here anymore, but I am," I said, my throat tightening. "So... let one question float on my behalf, across this universe. *To her.*"

Her glow shifted, contemplative. "You know the answer isn't hers to give... don't you?"

"I know," I said softly, surrendering.

"What question?" she asked, her voice fading to an echo, like the last note of a song already slipping away.

I stared into the void—the nothingness between us that somehow held everything.

Then, softly, almost like a prayer, I whispered:

Why Am I?

Afterword

The book is finally over. If you're wondering whether I can say anything without a smirk, well, here's my attempt at sincerity. Be warned—it isn't exactly my natural habitat.

Writing a book demands discipline—something I've avoided my entire life. My interests are fleeting, intense but short-lived. For a couple of months, I'm consumed, and then it's all gone. This book exists because I trapped myself into a two-month timeline. Just long enough to write something meaningful, yet short enough to outpace my distractions.

When I started this book, I wasn't even sure I'd finish it. But somewhere along the way, it stopped feeling like I was writing and started feeling like I'd been kidnapped—duct tape over my mouth, thrown in the trunk, with the book flooring it to God knows where. I kicked, I screamed, I procrastinated. It didn't care.

"Satire is jaggery on bitter quinine—it slips an unwanted truth down the throat of an unsuspecting buffalo," Maa told me this when I was ten. I never quite figured out the buffalo part, but the lesson stuck. Satire cuts deepest when it sneaks in with a smile. For me, satire isn't just a tool. It's the only way I see the world. It's a filter I can't turn off.

My first encounter with satire—at the ripe old age of ten— was through street theater. I acted in *Janata Paagal Ho Gayi Hai* (The Public Has Gone Mad), a play by Shivaram. That's when it clicked: comedy and critique weren't separate things. They fed off each other. The play's dialogues were written entirely in poetry, with five characters embodying all of India.

It was creative liberty at its peak—a privilege I fully exploited while writing this book.

A few years later, I went to Prof. Rajesh Mohan to learn music. The man heard me sing, winced like he bit into a lemon, and immediately rerouted me to poetry instead. An act of mercy? Or did he just sense that my true talent lay in ruining people's days through poetry? Poetry, he said, wasn't just an art, but a weapon. And he showed me how to wield it.

I've ripped off inspiration shamelessly from everywhere. *Raag Darbari* by Shrilal Shukla, *Urdu ki Aakhiri Kitaab* by Ibn-e-Insha, Rashomon by Kurosawa, Animal Farm by George Orwell. This book is stitched together from the fingerprints of better artists who showed me what's possible. And then there's Mel Brooks and Ricky Gervais, who taught me that we're all just cosmic jokes wrapped in flesh.

Someone told me to read Terry Pratchett, but by then, my first draft was already done. Too late. I picked up *Small Gods*, got five pages in and instantly knew I'd missed a masterclass. It was like discovering fire… right after you finished cooking on wet twigs. I wish I had read him more before writing this book. If you spot a faint Pratchett-esque glimmer here and there, now you know why.

For the right audience, philosophy is its own brand of humor. Kabir, Osho, and Gibran handed me wisdom wrapped in punchlines. As for the poets—too many to name—they all taught me that truth is funniest when it bites.

At its heart, this book is an homage to all those influences. You might think I'm name-dropping to sound smart. But that's just confusing my gratitude with my greatness. That one's on you. Seriously.

This book exists because of a lot of people. And also—despite them. Writing is lonely. No one else sat at the desk staring at the blinking cursor, wondering if I should just quit and take up beekeeping instead. At least bees don't need rewrites. Or editors. Or feedback sessions that begin with, "... You said this book was about testing."

But credit where it's due:

My wife and son cheered me on—mostly because they knew it was safer to let me write than to watch me pace the house, muttering to myself like a lunatic.

Jose and Vipul, my mentors, wrote those Forewords out of love. Or maybe just for the sheer sadistic pleasure of watching me sweat. Either way, respect. They're the kind of friends you don't leave alone with a mic at your wedding.

Pradeep somehow convinced me to write a book... *my* book. I don't know how he did it, but I suspect witchcraft. He'll probably call it his crowning achievement for the next decade, and honestly, I'd let him. He earned it.

Ramit and Jayapradeep—my lifelong friends, ruthless critics. They called out my nonsense and kept me from chickening out. They stood by me throughout this journey, reading through endless drafts. I owe them more than gratitude. I owe them eternal rights to mock me for every unreadable draft they endured. And trust me, there were many.

Pallavi, Udita and Pavitra provided me timely and detailed feedback. Annoyingly decent people. Why are you so kind? You're ruining cynicism for the rest of us.

I always knew this book wouldn't have a big audience. Thank you for reading. Satire itself is a niche, and a satirical novel on testing? That's straight-up reckless. The tech world barely tolerates humor, let alone storytelling with teeth. We worship *thought leadership*, not thoughts that make us uncomfortable. I spent more time wrestling with the question, *"Is it worth it?"* than actually writing the book. In the end, mischief won. Self-doubt never stood a chance.

If you slogged through this cover to cover, we're grabbing chai. Paid for the book? The chai's on me—you earned it. Skipped straight to the Afterword? Forget chai, we're grabbing beer. You clearly need it more than I do.

I just hope there was one moment—just one—that made you pause and introspect. If there was, I'd love to hear your story... every bit of chaos is worth a conversation. If nothing resonated? Well, damn. That's rough. Either I totally screwed this up... or you've got the emotional range of a toaster. No judgment—alright, maybe a little—but seriously, not even *one* moment? We should talk.

And speaking of chaos...

Maa... this book is all I could manage. I followed your code of satire, but maybe I let the jaggery sink too deep in some places and let the bitterness cut too sharp in others. I can already hear your groans. And see your nods. Like you always said—*blame the chaos, not the cook.*

You understood my madness when no one else could.

You always have.

Love you.